Sidney W. Cornish

Short Notes on the Church and Parish of Ottery St. Mary Devon

SALZWASSER VERLAG

Sidney W. Cornish

Short Notes on the Church and Parish of Ottery St. Mary Devon

1st Edition | ISBN: 978-3-84605-910-4

Place of Publication: Frankfurt am Main, Germany

Year of Publication: 2020

Salzwasser Verlag GmbH, Germany.

Reprint of the original, first published in 1869.

SHORT NOTES

ON THE

CHURCH AND PARISH

OF

OTTERY ST. MARY,

DEVON,

COMPILED BY THE

REV. SIDNEY W. CORNISH, D.D.,

VICAR OF OTTERY ST. MARY.

EXETER :
WILLIAM POLLARD, 58, NORTH STREET.
C. D. MAYNE, BEDFORD STREET.
JOHN WARNE, OTTERY ST. MARY.
1869.

ENGLISH CHURCHES.

How beautiful they stand
Those ancient Altars of our native land !
Amid the pasture fields, and dark green woods,
Amid the mountain's clouds and solitudes ;
By rivers broad that rush into the sea,
By little brooks that with a lisping sound,
Like playful children, run by copse and lea,
Each in its little plot of holy ground,
How beautiful they stand
Those old grey Churches of our native land !

Our lives are all turmoil,
Our souls are in a weary strife and toil ;
Grasping and straining—tasking nerve and brain,
Both day and night for gain ;
We have grown worldly ; have made gold our God ;
Have turned our hearts away from lowly things,
We seek not now the wild flower on the sod ;
We see not snowy-folded angels' wings
Amid the summer skies ;
For visions come not to polluted eyes.

Yet, blessed quiet fanes !
Still piety, still poetry remains,
And shall remain, whilst ever on the air
One Chapel bell calls high and low to prayer—
Whilst ever green and sunny churchyards keep
The dust of our beloved, and tears are shed
From founts which in the human heart lie deep !
Something in these aspiring days we need
To keep our spirits lowly,
To set within our hearts sweet thoughts and holy.

MARY HOWITT.

TABLE OF CONTENTS.

APPENDICES.

Events of Local Interest in their Chronological Order.

SHORT NOTES

ON THE

PARISH & CHURCH OF OTTERY ST. MARY.

I. The parish of Ottery St. Mary is situate in the south eastern part of the county of Devon, in the valley of the Otter. The parish extends across the whole breadth of the valley to the summit of the high ground on either side, and is divided into two nearly equal parts by the river which takes a somewhat circuitous but still southerly course through it, and falls into the sea at a distance of about eight miles. Ottery St. Mary is a hundred of itself, co-extensive with the parish. The town stands nearly in the centre of the parish on the eastern bank of the river. Polwhele states that " the bounds of the manor and parish were taken by Sir George Yonge, Bart. (the lord of the manor), and the parishioners, by procession, on the 27th and 28th of November, 1776. The bounds are as ancient as King Edward the Confessor, being fixed by his royal charter, A.D. 1061."

II. Little is known of its early history. The oldest document which is extant in connection with the place is a Saxon charter, bearing date 1061, by which King Edward the Confessor granted the manor to the Chapter of the Cathedral Church of Rouen, in Normandy. This was confirmed by an inspeximus charter of King Henry III., A.D. 1269, which however is not to be found, the roll of that year being imperfect, but it is recited in a subsequent inspeximus by King Richard II. In Doomsday Book (vol. i, folio 104) the manor of Ottery St. Mary is described as held of the king by the Church of St. Mary, at Rouen, and is valued at a rental of sixty-six marks.

III. The first mention of any Church in the parish (which was co-extensive with the manor) occurs in the Register of Bishop Bronescombe, who consecrated a Church there on the Thursday following the Feast of St. Andrew, 1260. The towers are supposed to be the portion of that edifice, which was suffered to remain unaltered, when Bishop Grandisson made great alterations and additions about seventy-five years after.

IV. Early in the year 1335, John de Grandisson, Bishop of Exeter, entered into negociations with the Chapter of Rouen for the purchase of the manor and advowson, which was concluded on the 13th of June; and in 1337 he procured a Royal License from King Edward III. for the foundation of the College, and executed the foundation deed, which is a document of great interest, and shows the care and forethought and pious devotion with which that excellent prelate provided for the maintenance of the solemn worship of Almighty God, and the strict government of the College. The Parish Church was raised to the dignity of a Collegiate Church, the last Vicar, Oliver Fayrsey, being appointed to the office of minister in the new foundation.

V. In a letter addressed to Pope Benedict XII., Bishop Grandisson states that this Collegiate Church is dedicated to Our Lady and St. Edward the Confessor. It is impossible to ascertain, with any certainty, to what extent he interfered with the fabric as it stood in the time of Bishop Bronescombe, but it is thought that he built the choir and Lady Chapel east of the Towers, and retained the greater part of the walls and windows of the old Church to form the nave. It seems certain that he vaulted the whole Church anew, from the nodules in the nave, choir, aisles, and Lady Chapel, being ornamented with his arms and those of William de Montacute, Earl of Salisbury, who married his sister Katharine, and probably contributed towards the erection of the Collegiate Church The well known legend connected with the establishment of the Order of the Garter is said to refer to this noble lady.

VI. Under the foundation deed, the Collegiate body was to consist of forty members; the four principal of whom were the Warden, the Minister, the Precentor, and the Sacristan. To these were added four simple Canons for the service of the Church, eight choral Vicars in Priest's orders, one Priest to have charge of the Parishioners, one to celebrate the Morning Service, "Presbyter Matutinus," one Priest attached to our Our Lady's Chapel, eight Clerks called Secondaries, two other Clerks called Clerici Ecclesiæ, two others called Aquebajuli, whose duty it was to carry the vessels of holy water in processions and benedictions, eight Choir Boys, and a Master of grammar. Each of the Prebendaries had a house assigned to him in the Close, and a suitable residence was provided for the Choral Vicars and inferior Ministers where they lived in common.

VII. With such a staff of Clergy and inferior Ministers, it cannot be questioned but that the Services of the Collegiate Church would be conducted with great care and solemnity. The Use of the Cathedral Church of the diocese was, of course, followed ordinarily, but Bishop Grandisson provided for his Collegiate

Church a *usus* of its own on certain occasions, when he orders (in the seventh statute) the Divine office to be performed, "*secundum ordinale et consuetudinarium quæ eis fecimus et extraximus ex Exoniæ et Sarum usibus.*"

VIII. Ample provision was made in the way of endowment for the due support of this large ecclesiastical foundation; but it would occupy too much space to set it forth in all its details. It is enough to state that competent judges have estimated that the amount of property of which the College was despoiled at the Reformation, independent of the great tithes which were bestowed on the Dean and Canons of Windsor, would have produced an income of at least £10,000 a year at the present time.

IX. A list of the fifteen Wardens of the College is given by Dr. Oliver in his *Monasticon*; of whom the most distinguished was Thomas Cornish (1490-1511), who was Suffragan Bishop of Tyne to Fox, Bishop of Bath and Wells, and to Hugh Oldham, Bishop of Exeter. He held also, at the same time, the Provostship of Oriel College, Oxford (1493-1507). On the resignation of his wardenship, he was appointed Precentor, Chancellor, and Canon Residentiary of Wells, where he died, and was buried near the door of the Chapter House of the Cathedral in 1531. Another Warden, Thomas Chard (1513-1518), Bishop of Solubria, was also coadjutor to Bishop Oldham and Bishop Veysie. The only Prebendary of note was Alexander Barclay, the author of the English version of *Navis Stultifera*, a metrical satire on the follies of the age. It is a translation from a German work written by Sebastian Brandt, of Strasburgh, entitled, *The Narrenschiff*, or Ship of Fools. Barclay seems to have made considerable interpolations in the original work; as for instance, in one part he calls on the fools to make way for the eight secondaries of the Church of St. Mary of Ottery, who deserve the first benches in the vessel:

> "Soft, foolis, soft, a little slack your pace,
>   'Till I have space you to order by degree;
> I have eyght neyghbours that first shall have a place
>   Within this my shyp, for they most worthy be;
> They may their learning receyve costles and free,
>   Their walles abutting and joining to the schooles,
> Nothing they can, yet nought will they learn nor see,
>   Therefore shall they guide this one Shyp of Fooles."

And again, in speaking of the ignorance of the clergy of his day, he says—

> "For if one can flatter, and beare a hawke on his fist,
>   He shall be made parson of Honington or of Clyst."

Barclay is chiefly remembered as the first writer of eclogues in the English language. He died in 1552, Rector of Allhallows, London.

X. The obits kept in the College were as follows :

January 9.   Nicholas Braybrook and Sir Theobald Mountenay.
February 11. Peter de Pateshulle,* Treasurer of Exeter Cathedral.
April 2.   Otho de Grandisson, uncle of the founder.
April 23.   Katharine Montacute, sister of the founder.
May 17.   Peter, Cardinal Bishop of Preneste.
May 20 and 21.   Sir Otho de Grandisson, brother of the founder.
June 3.   Edward, the Black Prince.
June 4.   William de Grandisson, Archdeacon of Exeter, brother
    of the founder.
June 5.   William Parochus.
June 27.   William de Grandisson, father of the founder.
July 14.   Thomas de Grandisson, brother of the founder.
August 26.   Thomas Byttelisgate and Jane his wife.
October 11.   Sibilla de Grandisson (formerly Sibilla Tregoz), mother
    of the founder.
October 27.   Peter de Courtenay, Esquire.
November 26.   John Prestocoote.
December 2.   Thomas Brantyngham, Bishop of Exeter.
December 10.   Agnes de Northwode, the founder's sister.
December 10.   Pope John XXII.

XI. This may be the most convenient place to call attention to
the emblazonments on the ten shields which ornament the cornice
of the Altar screen, in connection with Bishop Grandisson and
his contemporaries. We are indebted to the late James Pulman,
Esq., Yeoman-Usher of the Black Rod, for the following description of them in their order.

1.   The arms of Sir Otho de Grandisson, brother of the founder.

2.   The arms of Sir John de Northwode, who married Agnes,
the founder's sister.

3.   The arms of Sibella, wife of William Lord Grandisson, and
mother of the founder.

4.   The arms of Blanche de Mortimer, who married Peter Lord
Grandisson, the founder's brother.

5.   The royal arms of France, set up in honour of Isabel, Queen
Dowager of Edward II., and daughter of Philip IV., King of
France, in whose right her son, Edward III., claimed to be King
of France.

6.   The royal arms of England, as borne by Edward III., who
assumed the title of King of France about 1337.

7.   The arms of John de Grandisson, Bishop of Exeter, and
founder of the Collegiate Church.

8.   The arms of William de Montacute, Earl of Salisbury, the
husband of Katherine Grandisson.

9.   The arms of Peter de Courtenay, Standard Bearer to King
Edward III., Governor of Windsor Castle, and Lord Chamberlain,
the companion of the Black Prince in his wars in France and Spain.

10.   The arms of William Lord Grandisson, the father of the
founder.

* Probably a near kinsman of Sir John de Patteshulle, who married Mabill, sister
of the founder.

XII. The College was dissolved by King Henry VIII., and its endowments alienated in 1545. The manor was granted to Edward Seymour, Earl of Hertford, afterwards Duke of Somerset and Lord Protector, who was attainted and executed in the following reign, 1552. It then reverted to the Crown, and was held by it until it was sold by King Charles I. in the fourth year of his reign. By the directions of the will of King Henry VIII., his son and successor granted the appropriations, great tithes, and other endowments held by the College to the Dean and Canons of Windsor. The small tithes of the parish, together with the Church, Churchyard, and messuages and houses formerly occupied by the Vicar, Secondaries, Choristers, and School, were assigned to a Church corporation, established by letters patent of King Henry VIII. (dated December 24, anno regni xxxvii.), under certain trusts set forth in their Charter of Incorporation. The original Charter is lost, but there is extant in the Rolls' Office an inspeximus in the sixteenth year of Queen Elizabeth. In the fifth year of Edward VI., a suit having been commenced against the Corporation in the Court of Augmentations, a compromise was made between the parties to the suit, with the sanction of the Court, by which "eight of the most honest, best, discreetest and quietest of the parishioners" were to be associated with the Governors as their assistants, in dealing with all financial questions, and from them the future Governors were to be appointed.

The right of presentation to the Vicarage was retained by the Crown, and is exercised by the Lord Chancellor.

XIII. We cannot do better than introduce strangers to the architecture of the Church with the brief description given of it by Mr. Rickman, who visited it early in the present century.

"*Ottery St. Mary.*—This is a large and curious Church, being built like Exeter Cathedral with two towers for transepts. The Church consists of nave and aisles, choir and aisles, and a Lady Chapel. The greatest part of the edifice is Early English, of a character rather different from what is common, and having various small alterations of later date. The exterior is plain, and the windows are mostly without drip stones. At the east end of the Lady Chapel are some good niches of later date than the Chapel itself. The groining of the interior is of later date than the building; and the north aisle is of Perpendicular character and late date, with a very rich roof, ornamented with pendants. In this Church is a very rich monumental arch over an altar tomb which is plain, but has an effigy of an armed knight. This arch has fine mouldings and hanging tracery, with an ogee canopy, with crockets and a large finial. Over the whole of this monument shields are intermixed with the foliage in great numbers, and in a mode not very common. On the whole this Church deserves very minute examination."—Rickman's *Architecture in England*, 4th edition, London, 1835, p. 154.

XIV. It is remarkable that "so careful and accurate an observer" (for so Mr. Rickman is designated by Mr. J. H. Parker in his *Introduction to Gothic Architecture*) should have noticed only the monumental arch on the north side of the nave, and the recumbent figure of Sir Otho de Grandisson, to whose memory it was erected, and omitted its exact counterpart on the south side, beneath which is the figure of Beatrix his wife, with dogs at her feet, the usual emblem of fidelity. Both of them, indeed, were very much blocked from view by high pews, and the upper portion of the southern arch had been shamefully cut away, in order that a gallery might be carried over it, and partly supported by what was suffered to remain. This wilful damage was happily repaired at the restoration of the Church in 1850. Mr. Blore, who superintended the restoration of the reredos in 1832, pronounced them to be unsurpassed by any monuments of the same character in the kingdom.

XV. The only important addition to the fabric, as it was left by Bishop Grandisson, is the north or Dorset aisle. There are strong grounds for fixing the date of its erection between the years 1504 and 1530. Apart from its architectural character, in the porch are the arms of Bishop Oldham, who presided over the See of Exeter, 1504—1519; and on one of the corbels within the aisle are the arms of Bishop Veysey, who succeeded him 1519-1551.

On reference to the court rolls of the manor of Ottery, it appears that the ancient mansion and estate of Knightstone passed, on failure of the issue of the family of Bittlesgate, to Cicely, the only daughter and heiress of William Lord Bonvill. In 1494 the homage present the death of Richard Bittlesgate, and that the right descended to Thomas, Marquis of Dorset and Cicely his wife, in right of the said Cicely. Thomas Grey, Marquis of Dorset, died in 1501, and in 1503 she married Henry Stafford. In 1523 is presented the death of Henry Lord Stafford (created Earl of Wiltshire), who held the premises in right of Cicely his wife, and in 1530 her death is presented. The Stafford knot is a frequent device in the moulding below the parapet on the external walls of the aisle in question. Connecting this fact with the possession of Knightstone, and her well-known liberality in adding to the Churches of parishes in which she possessed property, no further evidence can be required to show that it was erected by Cicely, Countess of Wiltshire and Marchioness of Dorset.

XVI. One of the most remarkable features of the Church is the adaptation of the towers to form the arms of the transept. This portion of the Church was apparently erected *previous* to the same design being adopted in Exeter Cathedral, rather than constructed afterwards in imitation of it. Bishop Quivil (1280-1291) we know, conceived and executed the bold design of constructing a transept there out of the massy towers of Bishop Warelwast, taking down the inner side of each to nearly half its height from the ground, and constructing vast and substantial arches to sustain the upper, remaining, part. However this may be, it is supposed that there is no other example of a like arrangement in this country. (Appendix A.)

XVII. The dimensions of the Church:

	ft.	in.		ft.	in.
Extreme length from East to West	163	6	Breadth of Lady Chapel -	18	0
Length of Nave - -	66	0	Length of Dorset Aisle -	54	9
Length of Transept - -	79	0	Breadth of Dorset Aisle -	19	6
Breadth of Transept - -	18	0	Height of Vaulted Roof in Nave - - -	34	0
Length of Choir - -	59	0	Height of Towers to Battlements - - -	64	0
Breadth of Nave and Choir with Aisles - -	40	6	Ditto to top of Pinnacles -	71	0
Length of Lady Chapel -	20	6	Spire of Cock Tower, additional	30	0

XVIII. All the painted windows at present in the Church are of recent date, the earliest having been put up as lately as 1843. Risdon in his *Survey of Devon* (written between the years 1605-30) thus describes the condition of the Church in his time, " Otery Church is fair, according to the structure of those times; whereof the windows, little and low, are so bedecked with the armories of divers benefactors, more especially of the founders, that instead of ' Lux fiat ' it may be verified that they are umbrated thereby." It may fairly be assumed, therefore, that these windows, from not containing subjects which were deemed superstitious, escaped injury during the Puritan visitation of 1559, and were wantonly destroyed by the impious invaders of the sanctuary, when it was occupied by the Parliamentary forces in 1645. Looking at the long connection of the Church with Rouen in early times, it is not unlikely that the ancient glass had been supplied from that city, as was the case at Exeter Cathedral, where we learn from the fabric rolls of 1317-18, a large quantity of glass, both plain and coloured, was imported from Rouen, and landed at Seaton; the former at 4d. per foot and the latter at 8d. Risdon's account of the Church is confirmed by reference to *The Roll of Arms collected from the Churches and Houses of the Nobility and Gentry of the County of Devon, in the reign of Elizabeth*, where it appears that all the armorial bearings on the cornice of the Altar, as well as numerous other armorial decorations, then extant in Ottery Church, were therein set forth in colours. (*Communicated by Mr. Pulman, in* 1832.)

A list of the subjects of the several windows, with the names of their respective artists, will be found in the Appendix (B).

XIX. The Collegiate Church was, without doubt, maintained in all the beauty of holiness (as it was left by its munificent founder) during the two centuries which intervened between the foundation of the College and its dissolution (A.D. 1337-1545). But the work of confiscation then began; although no records remain whereby to trace its progress. Instead of eight bells, four in each tower (for the tolling and chiming of which such minute directions were given in the Grandisson Statutes), the inventory of Church goods taken in 1553 shows that there was but " one greate bell " in the parish Church of Ottery St. Mary; and the oldest bell, in the present peal of six, bears the date of 1652. Then followed the mutilation of the Altar screen and other ornaments of the Church by Queen Elizabeth's visitors about 1559; of whose operations here we may form some idea by reference to their doings at Exeter, where "they defaced, and pulled down, and burnt in the Cathedral yard, all the images and monuments they can find, and among other things defaced the Altars." Popular tradition in the neighbourhood ascribes these acts of violence to the troopers of Fairfax, when they were quartered here in 1645 ; but the date of 1603 (the year of the accession of King James I.) on the plaster Altar piece shows that they are free from this charge. The Rebellion has enough else to answer for touching the desecration of the Churches. To that eventful period may be ascribed the wholesale destruction of the painted windows with which our parish Church was so profusely adorned, and the destruction of the organs in the Church and Lady Chapel, and of the substantial benches throughout the nave, with their exquisitely carved ends, of which some specimens are still preserved in the Dorset Chapel. These probably were cleared away to make room for the Parliamentary troops and their horses (which were quartered in the Church during the occupation of the town in 1645), and might have served for fuel during the bleak month of November, while pestilence was thinning their ranks, until the prevailing sickness, which was aggravated by the want of sufficient accommodation, at length compelled them to remove to Tiverton. There is no historical record of the doings of the miserable thirty-five days during which the town was at the mercy of these unwelcome visitors ; but as the same parties formed a portion of the army to which Exeter surrendered in the following April, it will be doing them no injustice to quote their conduct there in shameful breach of the Articles of Treaty, in illustration of the indignities to which our Church was probably subjected.

"The Churches were plundered and applied to the most indecent purposes. The Chapter House they converted into a stable for their horses, and the Bishop's palace, the Deanery, and Canon's houses into barracks for the soldiers. Thirteen of the Parish Churches were exposed to sale by the public crier. The barbarians also demolished the beautiful stained glass in the windows of the Cathedral, defaced the sculptured ornaments, and especially the sepulchral monuments, and fired their muskets at the Altar piece, the marks of which are said to be still visible. In short they seem to have been subject to little restraint from any principle of decency, taste, honour, or humanity." It is not difficult to imagine what the feelings of the peaceful inhabitants of Ottery must have been, when they witnessed the ruin and desecration of the "holy and beautiful house" in which their fathers had praised God. How must they have been ready to take up the Lamentation of the Prophet : "I am pained at my very heart ; my heart maketh a noise in me ; I cannot hold my peace, because thou hast heard, O my soul, the sound of the trumpet, the alarm of war ! Destruction upon destruction is cried, for the whole land is spoiled ! "—*Jeremiah* iv., 19, 20.

XX. Long before the breaking out of the civil war, the nave had begun to be disfigured with galleries ; on one of which, immediately over the entrance north of the great western doors, ran this inscription. "Ended the 10 day of October, Ano Domini, 1606, G. C.

W. C., I. S. In front of the gallery in the south aisle (for the purpose of whose erection, a portion of the beautiful canopy over the tomb of Beatrix de Grandisson was ruthlessly cut away) the perpetrator of the deed was not ashamed to affix his initials in claim of the achievement.

" Erected by I. V., 1658."

Three other galleries were erected in after years, one in the north transept, and two, one over the other, in the south. The ancient seats and carved bench ends were replaced by hideous high pews, and, towards the close of the last century, the stone screen which separated the nave and Chancel was taken down, and the Chancel, which was previously arranged with twelve of the ancient misereres on either side, was pewed throughout, and the old stalls relegated to the north and south walls of the Chancel aisles ; to be restored under happier auspices to the place of honor which they had so fitly held in bygone generations. No trace or record remains of any ancient pulpit ; but the present one bears the inscription, " Richd. Marker, Clerk, M.A., Churchwarden, 1722," and below " All this in every part was done by me Wm. Culme, born in this parish." There is an old story told respecting the builder, that after its erection he went into foreign parts, where he saw much superior work ; and on his return was so dissatisfied with his performance that he offered to replace it with one of better workmanship, but the parishioners declined his proposal.

XXI. During the last century, and the early portion of the present, the parish of Ottery St. Mary was no exception, in regard to the indifference which prevailed as to the decency of Divine worship, and the necessity of providing for the spiritual wants of the rapidly increasing population of the country. But a happier state of things was at hand. The first step towards the improvement of the Church was the restoration of the mutilated Altar screen, which was completed in 1833, by voluntary contributions, under the superintendence of Mr. Blore. This was followed by the mortuary window at the west end of the Dorset Chapel in 1843. Meanwhile, the district Churches of St. John the Evangelist at Tipton, and St. Philip and St. James at Escot, were built and endowed (A.D. 1840) ; the former by voluntary contributions, aided by the Incorporated and Diocesan Church Building Societies ; the latter at the sole charge of Sir John Kennaway, to whom the patronage of the benefice was assigned by the Ecclesiastical Commissioners. Six years later (1846), the Church of St. Michael the Archangel, West Hill, was built and partially endowed by voluntary contributions. These three Churches provided accommodation for above 700 worshippers in the distant portions of the parish ; and this increase of Church room fully justified the subsequent removal of the many galleries with which the parish Church was disfigured.

XXII. In the summer of 1841, some members of the Exeter Diocesan Church Architectural Society visited the Church, and " its general character as a fine structure of the Early English and Decorated styles (although comprising various alterations of later date) with the antiquity of its foundation, and the peculiar interest excited from its having been once a Collegiate establishment of importance, determined the Society to make it the subject of their first publication."

The great question of the restoration of the Church had long been uppermost in the minds of those whose zeal and liberality finally brought the work to a conclusion, and the public interest in the subject doubtless received a great impulse from that authentic record of its past history and present condition.

XXIII. What that condition was, it is difficult at this distance of time to realize. "To those who have ever seen it no words are wanted, and to those who have not, I should be suspected of exaggeration in giving the coldest and simplest account of what I must call the disgraceful state of the interior. No offensive form of pew or gallery was unrepresented in the Church; and in some instances a boldness of conception and execution was to be found, worthy of better subject matter than pew architecture. In one instance a beautiful canopy was cut off to support a gallery; in a second, a sort of pulpit was entered through another pew, the seat of which shut down over the door and steps of the pulpit, and held its inmates prisoners; in a third the pew was approached by a ladder, which the occupants drew up after them, like Robinson Crusoe, when they were safely ensconced, to allow the west door of the Church to open properly. It was of more serious consequence that the poor had been practically thrust out of the Church that belonged to them, or confined within such narrow and inconvenient limits, that attention was almost out of the question, and devotion impossible. The general arrangements of the Church were, in fact, utterly opposed to the decencies of worship; and few persons, I suppose, are inclined to doubt, that with the decencies much of the spirit and reality are inevitably banished. Common sense would lead us to expect this, and the Church of Ottery St. Mary was a practical proof of it."—*(From a Paper read before the Exeter Diocesan Architectural Society on the Restoration of the Church, by Sir John Duke Coleridge, Sep.* 11, 1851.*)*

XXIV. The project of the restoration commenced with the munificent offer, on the part of Sir J. T. Coleridge (to whose influence and liberality, aided by the zealous co-operation of his family and friends, the parishioners are indebted for the carrying out of the whole design), to restore the Dorset Chapel at his own expense. The determined opposition of a pew holder, however, proved for a time an insuperable objection. But this partial failure resulted at last in entire success; and after long negociations, and patient conflict with prejudices and difficulties, the whole Church was committed to Mr. Butterfield for internal restoration and rearrangement. Meanwhile, the restoration of the Lady Chapel, which included the reconstruction of the rood loft, was in progress, from designs furnished by Mr. Woodyer, in happy accordance with the larger works afterwards executed by Mr. Butterfield. It would occupy too much space, in these "Short Notes," to go into all the details of those larger works, and it is unnecessary, inasmuch as the whole subject has been ably set forth by Sir J. D. Coleridge, in the interesting Paper read by him before the Exeter Diocesan Architectural Society. A careful perusal of that Paper is recommended to all who desire to obtain a full and exact account of the manner in which Mr. Butterfield, by his professional skill and true conception of Christian art, has reproduced, in much of its pristine dignity and stateliness, a Church "unsurpassed among other Churches of its size for the majestic austerity of its design," and the admirable simplicity of its construction.

The reader who has proceeded thus far in the history of the Sacred Edifice, through all its vicissitudes of fortune, from the grandeur of its original foundation, to the acts of mutilation and violence which marked the several stages of its decline, will not be displeased to conclude the narrative with an account of its reopening under happier auspices, compiled from several contemporary accounts of that event.

XXV. Some years ago the Church of Ottery St. Mary was celebrated almost equally as one of the noblest specimens of Early English architecture in the west of England, and as a building defaced, to a singular extent, by the irreverence of later days. The fabric itself, indeed, thanks to its own massive character, was unimpaired, and required no material restoration; but few Churches of equal beauty had been so entirely disfigured by the pews and galleries of our more immediate forefathers. In one very important particular also, the Church itself having been originally a *Collegiate* foundation was unsuited for the perfect celebration of *parochial* worship. Its design, like that of Exeter Cathedral, is cruciform with the unusual arrangement of two towers for the transepts. A second cross is also formed by lateral Chapels (now used as vestries) north and south of the sacrarium. It has also side aisles terminating eastward in Chapels, a Lady Chapel, and a large north-western Chapel of Perpendicular work, which forms, as it were, a second nave.

XXVI. Thus the original Chancel, designed for the Priests of the College founded by Bishop Grandisson, comprehended the transepts, the level of the nave extending only to their western limits. In consequence of this arrangement one half of the congregation was raised above the other, in defiance both of convenience and propriety, the reduced number of the Clergy (the present foundation only providing for a Vicar and Chaplain-Priest) being of course unable to occupy the space formerly allotted to their use. Mr. Butterfield, therefore, determined not only to bring the transepts to the same level with the nave, but to extend the latter eastward to the third bay from the reredos, reserving the remaining space for the Sacrarium, and a reduced Chancel commensurate with the requirements of the present Clergy and Choir. This step, which was much questioned as to its effect on the proportions of the Church when first proposed, has been attended with complete success in this respect, as well as in others more important. The whole space thus allotted to the congregation has been fitted with low open seats, stained, of a simple design; the few richly carved bench ends that remained in different parts of the Church, having been all brought together in the Dorset Chapel. The southern tower is given up to the organ, the ancient clock, and the belfry. The pulpit, desk, and eagle lectern are placed near to the south eastern pillar of the central dome. All the seats in the Church were intended to have been open, and to have faced eastwards; and were so shown in the original design. For the doors attached to certain of the seats, and for the arrangement of the seats, facing north and south to the east of the transept, the Corporation are responsible, as it was a condition absolutely imposed by them upon the architect and promoters of the restoration, but not to be defended for a moment as an architectural or devotional arrangement.

XXVII. The Chancel is occupied with twelve stalls, returned, formed from some of the ancient misereres, and fronted with panels of the ancient carvings. In front of them are placed the boys of the Choir. A screen of oak, not rising above the backs of the returned stalls (without gates) separates the Chancel from the nave; and the ancient rood-screen has been fixed under the bays immediately east of the stalls, shutting out the side aisles from the open space in front of the Sacrarium. This is inclosed by a low Altar rail of a very beautiful design, and within it stands the Altar, on a raised foot-pace, large and simple, the frame-work being composed of the old wood of the Church, and the top a slab of Portland stone. The whole of the aisles, Chancel, and Sacrarium are laid with encaustic tiles of various patterns, increasing in richness and variety as they approach the Altar.

XXVIII. The Chapels of St. Lawrence and St. Stephen, at the end of the north and south aisles of the Chancel, have been thoroughly restored and adorned at the sole expense of the Rev. R. H. Podmore, the Chaplain Priest. They are fitted up for private devotion or meditative retirement, whenever the time shall come that our Anglican Churches shall be free of access at all hours of the day, and not only during the time of Common Prayer. The Lady Chapel has also been most carefully restored (from a design by Mr. Woodyer), and fitted up for daily Morning Prayer. The Altar, which stood heretofore in the Chancel, has been placed here; some stalls are arranged for the Clergy, and the portion of the Chapel under the rood-loft, with the ambulatory, fitted with solid oaken benches for the congregration.

XXIX. The vaulting of the entire Church, with the exception of the Dorset Chapel, has been decorated with colour. In the transepts and side aisles the ribs only have been painted, and the bosses, as throughout the Church, gilded. These last are of remarkable beauty along the central line of the Chancel vaulting, where a series of sacred subjects is represented in them, consisting of figures of St. John Baptist, St. Anne teaching the Blessed Virgin, the Annunciation, the Holy Mother and Child, and SS. Joseph and Mary. In the rest of the Church, the ground-work between the ribs has also been coloured. This decoration increases in brilliancy as it passes eastwards, and is lavished with much splendour over the Chancel and Sacrarium. The cornice, central canopy, and entire lower stage of the reredos, have also been adorned with colour and gilding, as well as the ancient wooden screen between the side aisles and Chancel before mentioned. The Chapels of SS. Stephen and Lawrence are adorned with golden stars on a deep blue ground, and their ribs and bosses exquisitely painted. The same kind of ornament is used with great effect in the Lady Chapel.

XXX. The contract for the wood-work throughout the Church was taken by Mr. Livermore, Builder; that for the mason's work in the nave, choir, and transepts, by Mr. Digby; and that for the Dorset Chapel and Lady Chapel, by Mr. Selway—all of them tradesmen of Ottery St. Mary, and their work throughout has been executed with skill and fidelity. Great credit also is due to Mr. John Baker, another deserving inhabitant of the town, who has displayed much skill and ability in the embellishment of the roof, which may fairly challenge comparison with anything of the kind in the west of England.

XXXI. When our readers call to mind the extent and difficulty of the works connected with this restoration, they will be surprised to hear that they were completed in less than twelve months. During the whole work, extending over every portion from the pavement to the roof, the Church was open for three full Services every Sunday, and the Daily Prayer was only suspended for a single week; a temporary wall of brick having been erected between the nave and transepts, and one half of the Church used for Divine Service, while the other half was under restoration.

XXXII. On Wednesday, the fifteenth day of May, 1850, within the Octave of the Feast of the Ascension, being the day appointed for the celebration of the accomplishment of the restoration of the Church, there was a goodly gathering of Clergy and Laity interested in the work, within its walls, attracted by the fame of the structure itself, and of the pains which had been taken to render it more worthy of the service of Almighty God. The weather was most favourable, and the noble peal of bells struck up at four o'clock in the morning to herald in a day of unbroken loveliness. Many of the residents had arranged not to be present at the Morning Service, in order to allow room in their Church for the numerous strangers from a distance who would have to return home before the Afternoon Service. Before eleven o'clock the Church was crowded, the seats to the east of the pulpit, between it and the Choir, being reserved for the Clergy, of whom upwards of 100 were present. The Chancel was occupied by the Clergy of Ottery St. Mary and its district Churches, with the Bishop of Guiana (who specially suspended

his labours in the course of a Confirmation tour for the Bishop of
Bath and Wells), attended by the Rev. George Anthony Denison,
Archdeacon of Taunton, and the Rev. R. L. Webber as his Chaplains;
the Rev. Prebendaries Hole and Dornford ; the Rev. E. C. Lowe
and J. T. Boles, lately Curates in the parish. The Prayers were said
by the Rev. R. H. Podmore, the Chaplain Priest, and the Litany
by the Rev. G. E. Deacon, Assistant Curate of Ottery ; the First
Lesson was read by the Rev. E. C. Lowe, and the Second by the
Rev. A. A. Hunt. The Bishop of Guiana celebrated the Holy
Eucharist, the Vicar reading the Epistle, Archdeacon Denison
the Gospel, and Prebendary Dornford the Exhortation. The
Sermon was preached by the Rev. Prebendary Hole, from
1 Chronicles xxix., 13-15, "Now, therefore, our God, we thank
Thee, and praise Thy glorious Name. But who am I, and what
is my people, that we should be able to offer so willingly after
this sort? for all things come of Thee, and of Thine own have
we given Thee. For we are strangers before Thee, and sojourners,
as were all our fathers : our days on the earth are as a shadow,
and there is none abiding."

XXXIII. A Correspondent writing to the Editor of the *West of
England Conservative*, says, "I had the happiness of being present
at the reopening of Ottery Church on Wednesday last. A spectacle
more awakening and impressive it may not be my lot to witness;
in truth, the veriest enemy of our Holy Mother would, methinks,
have warmed in kindly mood, and must have confessed that the
Supreme was being worshipped in all the beauty of holiness.
More than 100 Clergy occupied the stalls and choir ; the nave and
aisles were filled with devout worshippers of the Laity, whose re-
verential conduct manifested a sense of the awful Being, in Whose
Presence they were assembled, and joy and gratitude that those
' haunts of sweet antiquity ' were restored and opened again for
Prayer and Praise. The Rev. Prebendary Hole preached a Sermon
which will live in the memories of all who heard it. It were injustice to its truthfulness in historical research—to its aptitude in
application—to its vivid portraiture of holy men long since gone
to their reward, and of holy living men, on whom God has bestowed
the privilege of re-edifying His sacred Fane—to its beauty in
chastened expression of a sorrowing heart for the loss of Him
who should have filled the Preacher's place (Bishop Coleridge)—
to its felicity of figures and allusions—its elegance of diction—its
practical appeal—its doctrinal truths—its powerful contrast between
the dogmas of the Anglican and Roman Churches—in those respects,
and many more, it were unjust to supply you with fragments of
this discourse which will be shortly published at the earnest request
of the Bishop and Clergy. At the conclusion of the Sermon the
Offertory was collected from the whole congregation, and amounted
to £100 (to be applied to the renewal of the clerestory windows in
the original Chancel), after which, the Holy Communion was ad-
ministered to above 200 Communicants, composed of Clergy and
Laity in about equal parts.

XXXIV. "Evening Prayer commenced at four p.m., when the Church was again well filled, and the places of those who had returned home were filled by the inhabitants of the town and neighbourhood. The Rev. Prebendary Dornford preached an appropriate and instructive Sermon from the Text, 'The poor have the Gospel preached to them'; in which he especially addressed himself to the parishioners on the privileges to which they were admitted by the Daily Services which are henceforth to be celebrated every morning and evening throughout the year, and on the responsibilities which such privileges bring with them. He alluded, with great felicity of expression, to the former state of the Church contrasted with its present magnificence, and to the labours and munificence of those through whose energetic exertions all the difficulties attendant on such an undertaking had been overcome, and this "House of God" restored not merely to a condition of decent comeliness, but to such ecclesiastical propriety and decorative splendour, as will scarcely be found again throughout the length and breadth of 'this fair English land.'

XXXV. "We should not omit to add that there was a congregational Baptism after the second lesson; at which, for the first time, the magnificent font, presented by Mr. Beresford Hope, was uncovered for use. It is massive in its proportion, of square Norman form, and supported by a central shaft and four smaller ones at the corners. The bowl and central shaft are of marble from the Ipplepen quarries, near Newton Abbot, and the block on which it rests is black marble from Plymouth. The four corner shafts are serpentine, from Helston; the mosaics on the side of the bowl are of Ipplepen marble, and black and red marbles from Plymouth; all the materials of which the font is composed being the product of the diocese except the white pieces which are foreign, as they cannot be procured of the required purity in England.

XXXVI. "In rendering our acknowledgements to those survivors who have been spared to 'bring on the headstone with shoutings,' it must not be forgotten that two of the foremost contributors to the great work have been called to their reward in the short interval which has elapsed since the restoration was projected, viz., the simple-hearted and munificent Vicar of St. Mary Church, and the honoured Warden of St. Augustine's College. In the mysterious dealings of God's Providence they assisted in sowing the seed, but have not been permitted, in the 'Church Militant here on earth,' to take their part in the joy of the harvest. The former, by especial desire, first introduced the subject to the parishioners, and pledged himself to one-tenth .of the whole expense. The latter, had his valuable life been spared, would have preached on Wednesday last, and taken his part in celebrating the conclusion of that noble undertaking which his nearest kinsman had so auspiciously opened."

XXXVII. Another Correspondent who was present on the opening day expresses in the following terms the impression which its Services left upon his mind : "Thus ended a day long to be remembered, not only by the parishioners of Ottery St. Mary, who from day to day continually will have cause to be thankful for the good work now brought to a conclusion, but also by all whose happy privilege it was to assemble within those holy walls for Prayer and Praise, and Thanksgiving and Communion. They will carry away with them—some of them across the waters of the broad Atlantic—an enduring recollection of those solemnities, as a bright spot in their remembrance of the pure and simple Rites of their Mother Church in all the "beauty of holiness." And even in our own favoured Diocese, it is not too much to hope that the Order of its Services, in exact accordance with the requirements of the Church's laws, will commend them to the hearts and affections of her children."

XXXVIII. The visitor has now been informed of all the more important objects connected with the ancient state of the Church and its recent restoration. It remains only to direct his attention to some minor details which deserve notice. They are as follows:

1. The piscina on the south, and the aumbry on the north side of the Altar in the Lady Chapel, and those also in the side Chapels.

2. The gilded lectern in the Lady Chapel, coeval with the College, and bearing the arms of the founder.

3. The consecration crosses throughout the Church, thirteen on the outside and eight on the inside, where the Consecrating Bishop touched the walls with the Holy Chrism.

4. The faded frescoes on the back of the reredos.

5. Specimens of the ancient tiles inlaid in the ambulatory.

6. The four sedilia in the Lady Chapel, and the three within the Altar rails.

7. The north and south vestries, each with its parvise, which were probably intended as chambers for the Presbyter Matutinus; also the south porch and the north porch, with its parvise, and, originally, two chambers, one over the other.

8. The clock, designed to show the age of the moon, as well as the hour of the day, apparently of the same age as that in Exeter Cathedral.

9. The apertures in the vaulting to the number of 98. (Appendix C.)

10. The bronze eagle lectern in the nave, a cast from the celebrated brazen eagle in Lynn Church, Norfolk.

11. The curious little niche at the north west corner of the transept, where it is supposed that he, whose office it was to ring the early Matin bell, placed his lamp or candle.

12. The misereres in the choir and Lady Chapel, some bearing under the seat the arms of Bishop Grandisson.

13. The carved bench-ends in the Dorset Chapel of the fifteenth century work.

14. The three brasses to the memory of the Shermans near St. Stephen's Chapel.

15. The five-light windows in either transept, which had each originally an Altar under them.

16. The parcloses, north and south, separating the Chancel from the side aisles, formed from the woodwork of the antient screen.

17. The seven narrow lights over the arch above the rood loft.

XXXIX. There are no monuments in the Church which call for especial notice on the score of design, but the following inscriptions will be read with interest.

1.

On ledger-stones in the ambulatory, behind the reredos :

Hic jacet Oliverus Smyth, quondam custos hujus Collegii, qui obiit 4 die Aprilis, Anno Domini MDXLIIII.

2.

Hic jacet Magister Joannes Guderling, Preb. hujus Collegii, qui obiit XX Decembris, Anno Domini MCCCCCXXXII.

3.

On a ledger stone, bearing a Calvary cross, at the entrance of the Lady Chapel :

Under this stone lie the remains of John Coleridge, Batchelor of Arts, and formerly Vicar of this parish. Also of Anne, his wife.

4.

On a small brass plate near the door of the south vestry.

Infra reconduntur Cineres Reverendi Thomæ Gatchell, Artium Baccalaurei, et hujus Ecclesiæ Vicarii; qui obiit decimo quarto diè Julii, Anno Dom. 1713.

5.

On an Altar-tomb on the north side of the Sacrarium :

Hic jacet Johannes Haydon de Cadhay, Armiger, et Johanna uxor ejus, consanguinea et heres Johannæ Cadhay, quæ fuit uxor Hugonis Grenvile generosi. Qui quidem Johannes fuit primus Gubernator incorporatus hujus Parochiæ, et obiit sine exitu nono die Martii, Anno Domini 1587. Dicta autem Johanna obiit sine exitu decimo nono die Decembris, Anno Domini 1592.

Pro quibus laus sit Deo.

6.

In St. Stephen's Chapel :   (Appendix M. 2).

On a father and son of the family of Sherman (resident at Knightstone), who both died on the same day, A.D. 1617.

Under this Monument lyes one
Did good to many, hurt to none,
Friended the rich, relieved the poor,
Was kind to all—Who can do more ?
That loved Hospitality,
And loathed Prodigality ;
That rais'd his State and Portion,
Yet used no oppression.
Each dweller and each tenant roar'd
At such a neighbour, such a Lord.
When aged weakness did possess
His crased body, nay the less
His steps his Church-path so would wear,
The Church should often have him there.
His limbs were weak, the walk was long,
Yet this seemed short, yᵉ other strong.
His life above, his death hereunder
Was full of goodness, full of wonder.
Six years beyond man's common age,
He walked here in Pilgrimage ;

C

18

And then one age, one very day,
Took both the Sire and Son away.
As if Time for the Sire and Son
As much as Time could do had done,
Making them live and die uneven,
And yet to live as Twins in Heaven.
Let us that are here standing by
Learn so to live and so to die,
That after Life and Death's annoy
We may revive and meet in joy.

7.

On Dorothy, his wife, sister to John Drake, of Ayshe, Esq.:

Within this monument doth also lye
A pattern true of our infirmitie :
Whose infancy, childhood, youth, and age
Was still attended by the wrathful rage
Of that which crept in by our Parent's fall.
Her welcome, entertainment, end, and all
Seemed all alike from first to latest breath,
She always seemed to die one living death.
Small griefs sometimes seeme great, but her's were so
As greater sielde* or never made less . . . .
These were her passions ; now her actions stood
Like the Samaritan's, entitled Good.
Had she a respite from her proper woe,
That day should respite other's pains also.
It was her custom and her comfort here,
As soon as her own rod did disappear
The comfortless to comfort, and restore,
According to her talent, sick and sore.
Hence envious Death did slay without remorse
Her that in others did withstand his force,
And pitiless to her no pity yielded
'Cause other's pains she pitiful relieved.
What need more words ?   Works shew her life was action,
Her dying words, her death was contemplation.
　　　She died the XXVII. August, 1620.

8.

On the wife of Gideon Sherman, Esq., daughter of Nicholas Fry, of Yarty, Esq., who died the first week after marriage, 1618.†

If wealth, wit, beauty, youth, or modest mirth
　Could hire, persuade, entice, prolong, beguile,
Death's fatal dart, this fading flowre on earth
　Might, yet unquailed, have flourished awhile,
But mirth, youth, beauty, wit, nor wealth, nor all,
Can stay, or once delay, when Death doth call.

No sooner was she to a loving mate
　From careful parents solemnly bequeathed,
The new alliance scarce congratulate,
　But she from him, them, all, was straight bereav'd ;
Slipping from bridal feast to funeral bere,
She soon fell sick, expir'd ; lies buried here,

---

* Used in *Piers' Plouhman,* in the sense of seldom.

† Our older inhabitants are wont to call to mind a somewhat similar warning of the instability of human happiness which happened here in the earlier part of this century, when Wm. Bagwell, Esq., of Ashcott, Somerset, was married, with all festive honors, to the Hon. Elizabeth Anne Graves, of Cadhay, and before two months had passed, the noble lady was brought back and laid in the Haydon vault, immediately under the Altar rail, where she had so lately knelt as a bride.

Oh, Death, thou mightest have waited in the field
  On murd'ring cannon, wounding sword and spear;
Or there, where fearful passengers do yield
  At every surge, each blast of wind doth rear;
In stabbing taverns, or infected towns,
On loathsome prisons, or on prince's frowns.

There not unlook't for many a one abides
  Thy direful summons; but a nuptial feast
Needs not thy grim attendance; maiden brides
  In strength and flower of age, thou may'st let rest.
With wings so weak mortality doth fly,
In height of flight death strikes, we fall and dy.

9.

At the foot of three brasses, fixed in a ledger stone near St. Stephen's Chapel, in memory of three members of the Sherman family.

ÆT MEMORIÆ

Joannis Sherman generosi, Gulielmi filii ejus, et Richardi nepotis qui, exipsorum voto, unà requiescunt.
Tres tegit hoc unum marmor: virtutibus omnes
  Ut tumulo, meritis, sanguine, laude pares.
Hic pater, hic natusque, neposque propagine clarâ
  Shermanni, Otræo, nomina clara solo,
Sancta Dei cultu, curâque celebria egenûm
  Queis pia subsidii híc munera in æva dabant.
Quilibet octo annos decies prope vixit, et aulâ
  Vivit jam æternâ spiritus orbe decus.
Híc unâ ex voto recubant; unâ inde resurgant,
  Ac unâ a Christo laurea pacta beet.
Johannes ob. 1542. Gulielmus ob. 1583. Richardus ob.

10.

Epitaphium Amicii Haydon filii Roberti Haydon, Armigeri, qui obiit 12 Januarii, An. Dom. 1614.
Quis jacet hic, quæris, percussus vulnere mortis?
  Virtutis socius nobilis, alter Ajax:
Mortuus, ah! dixi? revoco, sic esse videtur
  In cælis vivit nescius ille mori.

11.

Under the effigy of John Coke, of Thorn, Esq. (in the east end of the Dorset Chapel), who died March 28, 1632:

Nos simul ac orimur, morimur: Cocus inclitus urnâ
Conditur exiguâ populo peramabilis omni:
Vivit at ille tamen, quem sic lugetis ademptum,
Non obiit sed abivit; agit felicia cælo
Secula, nec tenui possit sub cespite claudi.

12.

Sara Haydon, filia Roberti Haydon, Armigeri, quæ obiit 24 Aprilis, An. Dom. 1620.*
Apollo moist this tomb with tears
For such great loss in tender years.
Virtue's hope now is dead,
And fro' Earth to Heaven fled.
Wit's perfection with pure spirit
Doth an Angel's place inherit.
Stay in that celestial skie,
Where thou shalt live and never die.

* The small slab on which these lines were engraved was in the north Chancel aisle, near the entrance to the vestry. It was so dilapidated that it fell to pieces on removal, and could not be put together again.

13.

Inscription over the south porch inside the Church:

In obitum ornatissimi Viri
Johannis Haydoni, Armigeri.
Vitâ defuncti carmen.

Dicite mortales, quis fructus Divitiarum
  Hinc cum demigrans vita petita fugit?
Dicite quam multum dives sit paupere major
  Cum fera Mors unâ tollit utrumque Die.
Omnis homo fœnum est, levis et vanescit ut umbra;
  Nulla est, et fœdis vermibus esca manet.
Indicat hoc nobis tua mors, Haidone, dolendi,
  Quæ siccas hominum non sinit esse genas.
In patriam Benefacta tuam permagna supersunt,
  Quæ poterunt multi multa referre Viri.
A Rege Henrico primus Diploma parasti
  Floreat ut literis læta juventa bonis;
Ludus ut erectus siet et Rectoria clara
  Effecit studium sedulitasque tua.
Sparsit ubique tuam pietatem Pons novus infra,
  Inque Deo monstrat Porticus ista fidem.
Legum cultor eras, semper dilectus egenis,
  Impia devitans jurgia, pacis amans.
Vos igitur pueri, juvenes properate senesque
  Et mecum Haydoni tradite corpus humo.
Illi, qui meruit Prœconia reddite justa,
  Funus et elegiis concelebrate suum.
Dicite, Livor abi; tandem post funera cessa,
  Spiritus Haydoni nam loca sancta tenet,
Qui multa in terris vivens benefacta locavit,
  Cum Christo sedem jam capit ille suam.

1618.

14.

The original door in the southern porch, which was built by John Haydon, still remains, and the iron handle bears the initials and date "I. H. 1571." The royal arms are within the porch above the doorway, with the following inscription over them:

He that no il will do
Do nothyng yt lang yto.
I. H.

Under the arms

In te, Domine, speravi,
Non confunder: in æternum.

15.

A spacious tablet on the western side of the porch contains an abstract of the bequests of Mr. Thomas Axe to this parish, of which his father, George Axe, was originally parish clerk, then registrar under the Commonwealth, and reappointed to his former office at the Restoration. (*Vide* Short Biographical Notices, No. 4.)

APPENDIX A.

The examples of transeptal towers on the Continent are very rare. In an article entitled "The Churches of Chartres and Le Mans" (*Saturday Review*, August, 1868, p. 257), the following observation occurs: "Little as the building seems to be known, the thirteenth century work at Le Mans undoubtedly entitles it to rank among the noblest Churches of the middle ages. The original design embraced *two towers at the end of the transept, like Exeter, Ottery, and seemingly, St. Martins at Tours.*"

———

APPENDIX B.

"Storied windows, richly dight,
Casting a dim religious light."

A list of the subjects of the several windows, with the names of of their respective artists, commencing with the west window in the Dorset Chapel.

1. The Apostles' window (*Wailes*). A mortuary window, erected by her brothers, "In memory of Frances Duke Patteson, wife of the Right Honourable Sir John Patteson, Knight, and only Daughter of James and Frances Coleridge, of this place. She deceased XXII Nov., MDCCCXLII."

2. The Transfiguration (*Warrington*). "An humble offering to Almighty God and His Church by Louisa, Lady Rolle, 1850."

3. The Nativity (*Wailes*). Subscribed for by the little children of the parish at the restoration of the Church.

4. King Solomon (*Preedy of Worcester*). Presented by G. H. Pattrick, Esq., in memory of Mr. F. G. Coleridge.

5. Isaiah and Ezekiel (*Wailes*).

6. Jeremiah and Daniel (*Wailes*).

7. St. Mark the Evangelist (*Wailes*).

8. St. Luke the Evangelist (*Wailes*).
These four windows were filled by subscriptions from old scholars of the King's School, who formerly occupied the gallery in the north transept.

9. Worship of the Lamb by the Church (*Hardman*).* Mortuary window to the memory of Frederick William Coleridge.

* "This is intended to symbolize the worship of the spotless Lamb by the whole Church, described in the 14th chapter of the Revelation, being the Epistle for the Holy Innocent's day. In the centre of the centre-light stands the Lamb on a mount, from which issue the four streams of Paradise. Over Him, in the same light, are

10. St. Titus *(*Warrington*).*
11. St. Timothy *(Warrington).*

} Presented by a friend through the Rev. R. W. James, Vicar of Southleigh.

12. St. Barnabas *(Warrington).*
13. St. Paul *(Warrington).*

} Mortuary windows erected in memory of Mr. T. B. Davy, by his sisters.

14. St. James the Great *(Warrington).*   Presented by Mr. Francis James Coleridge.

15. St Peter's Vision, Acts x., 2 *(Wailes).*

16. Cornelius and the Angel, Acts x., 3 *(Wailes).*

17. St. Paul raising Eutychus to life, Acts xx., 10 *(Wailes).*

18. St. Paul shaking off the viper, Acts xxviii., 5 *(Wailes).*

19. Martyrdom of St. Laurence* *(Hardman).*

20. Full length figure of St. Laurence *(Hardman).*

21. Healing of the nobleman's son, St. John iv., 50 *(Warrington).*   A thanksgiving window presented by T. C. Sneyd Kynnersley, Esq.

22. Little children brought to Christ *(O' Connor).*   A mortuary window, arranged from a picture by Overbeck.

23. A "Te Deum" window *(Hardman).*   Erected by numerous friends "in pious memory of Francis George Coleridge, A.D. 1855."†

24. St. John Baptist and his parents *(O' Connor).*   A mortuary window in memory of Rev. George Smith, Vicar of this Church (1794-1841), and his wife Elizabeth.

25. Raising of the ruler's daughter, St. Luke viii., 54 *(O' Connor).*   A thanksgiving window presented by Francis George Coleridge, Esq.

26. Full length figure of St. Stephen‡ *(Hardman).*

27. Martyrdom of St. Stephen, Acts vii., 58 *(Hardman).*

28. Baptism of the jailor and his family at Philippi, Acts xvi., 33 *(Wailes).*

29. St. Paul and Silas at Philippi, Acts xvi., 30 *(Wailes).*

30. St. Paul and his company entering the house of Philip the Evangelist, Acts xxi., 8 *(Wailes).*

31. Philip baptizing the Ethiopian eunuch, Acts viii., 38 *(Wailes).*

His parents—the Blessed Virgin and St. Joseph. Below Him St. John, His Forerunner, and St. Augustine, the first Archbishop of this province. The two lights on each side of the centre are filled with heads of Saints in pairs, one in each light, representing the different orders of the Church, and chosen, as far as possible, from English Saints : St. Agnes and St. Katharine for the virgins ; St. Mildred and St. Etheldreda for queens and abbesses ; St. Peter and St. Paul for apostles ; St. Benedict and St. Bernard for the religious orders, and St. Edward the Confessor the founder of Ottery St. Mary, and St. Edmund for the kings, martyrs, and confessors. The two outer lights are filled with angels holding scrolls inscribed with devotional texts." *(From Sir J. D. Coleridge's Paper on the Restoration of the Church, referred to in the preceding pages.)*

* St. Laurence was put to death by the heathen soldiers of the Emperor Valerian, for not surrendering the Church Treasury, which they thought was in his charge. They laid him on a gridiron and broiled him over a fire.

† "At the beginning the whole Church in Heaven and earth is described as occupied in that, for which all beings have been created—the service and praise of God. First, the pure spirits of God which never fell ; and next, the noblest of that race are pictured in their different states and conditions worshipping the Fountain of love, and light, and joy. . . Nor are the praises confined to the unseen world ; all the Church on earth, in its imperfect way, occupies itself in like manner. Nowhere do the strains of exulting praise rise higher ; we feel in singing it, as if we were singing our Creed." *(Commentary on the "Te Deum" by Bishop Forbes.)*

‡ Nos. 20 and 26 represent the two Deacon Saints of the Church. From designs by Pugin.

32. **Angel** window (*Wailes*). A mortuary window presented by Miss H. D. Coleridge.

33. **Unbelief** of St. Thomas, St. John xx., 27 (*Wailes*).

34. **Martyrdom** of St. Thomas* (*Wailes*).

35. **St.** Peter brought to Jesus by his brother St. Andrew, St. John i., 42 (*Wailes*).

36. **Crucifixion** of St. Andrew † (*Wailes*)

37. **St.** Michael the Archangel (*Hardman*). Presented by Rev. R. H. Podmore, the Chaplain Priest.

38. **Five** female Saints: St. Mary the Virgin, with the Blessed Infant; St. Anne, her mother, with the Blessed Virgin; St. Mary Magdalene; St. Mary, the mother of Cleopas, and St. Elizabeth, the mother of St. John Baptist (*Warrington*). Presented by the Rev. J. H. Randolph, Prebendary of St. Paul's Cathedral.

39. **St.** Gabriel the Archangel (*Hardman*). Presented by the Rev. R. H. Podmore.

Clerestory Windows.

40. **The** Circumcision (*Hardman*).

41. **The** Temptation (*Hardman*).

42. **The** Mocking (*Hardman*).

43. **The** Scourging (*Hardman*).

44. **The** Crucifixion (*Hardman*). Given by the young men and maidens of the parish.

45. **Christ** in Glory (*Hardman*). Given by some of the tradesmen of the town.

46. **The** Ascension (*Hardman*).

47. **The** Resurrection (*Hardman*).

48. **The** Transfiguration (*Hardman*).

49. **The** Adoration (*Hardman*).‡
    (40, 41, 42, 43, 46, 47, 48, 49, were presented by the Right Hon. Sir J. T. Coleridge).

50 and 51. Pattern Glass Windows in the Clerestory, behind the reredos (*Wailes*). Presented by F. G. Coleridge, Esq.

---

* There was a tomb not far from the city of Malipur (near the Ganges), whither the Apostle was wont to retire for his private devotions. Thither the Brachmans and their armed followers pursued him, and, while he was intent on prayer, they first loaded him with darts and stones, till one of them, coming near, ran him through with a lance.

† That his death might be made more lingering, he was fastened to the cross, not with nails, but with cords. The instrument of his martyrdom is said to have been in the form of the letter X, two pieces of timber crossing each other in the middle, and hence usually known as St. Andrew's Cross.

‡ The windows on the north side (numbered 40, 41, 42, 43, 44) represent subjects from our Lord's life in suffering; those on the south (45, 46, 47, 48, 49) from His life in glory.

APPENDIX C.

Apertures in the Vaulting of the Church.

Throughout the vaulting of the Church (with the exception of the Lady Chapel), there are no less than 98 apertures, several of which terminate in a leaden socket, evidently intended to serve some useful purpose connected with the fabric itself, or with the ceremonies of the Church. Mr. Markland, in a Paper read before the Architectural Society at Exeter (*Transactions*, vol. iv., p. 60-68), offers some suggestions as to their probable use. He says that wires or chains might have been transmitted through them for the suspension of lights and cressets, or tapestries and hangings on solemn occasions.

In Bishop Grandisson's Statutes there are numerous regulations touching the wax-lights, &c., and a large quantity was provided before Easter, but no particular description is given as to the mode of fixing the lamps or candles. They were usually employed in various Churches in large numbers for the Holy Sepulchre from Good Friday to Easter Day, and also in masses for the dead at the funeral of persons of distinction. In some Churches these apertures have occasionally been used for the purpose of passing ropes, by which workmen may be suspended instead of scaffolding in repairing or ornamenting the ceiling; but Mr. Butterfield inclines to the opinion that these apertures were for lights, and that the vaulting was treated in imitation of the vault of heaven ; and he notices the superior effect of light·thus coming above the level of one's eyes. These single lights were, probably, superseded by the subsequent introduction of chandeliers and coronas.

It is scarcely necessary to notice two other suggestions which have been offered—one, that they were for the purpose of ventilation, for which they were obviously inadequate ; and the other, that they were intended for drains to carry off the water which might lodge in the cavities of the groined ceiling while the Church was building, and before the outer roof was erected, for these apertures are found to run along, the centre of the roof, on which water could not rest. And certainly some plan would have been desired to carry it off externally; or, if required during the construction of the roof, they would scarcely have been suffered to remain when they were no longer needed for the purpose.

APPENDIX D.

*Battle at Feniton Bridge near Ottery St. Mary, in the reign of
King Edward VI., 27th July, 1549.*

"Honiton was made again the rallying point, and a tolerable
force was soon in arms there. As soon as Lord Grey should
come, the intention was to go forward immediately and fight a
battle under the walls of Exeter. [*That city was now besieged
by the insurgents*]. On the 27th July, scouts brought information that a body of Cornishmen were three miles off at Feniton
bridge. Their numbers were increasing, and they might hourly
be looked for at Honiton. A council of war was held, when Sir
Peter Carew [*of Mohuns Ottery*] was, as usual, for an instant
fight. His advice was taken; with as many as he could bring
together, Lord Russell went in search of the enemy, and found
them, to the number of a few hundreds, encamped in a meadow
across the river, below the bridge, waiting for a fresh detachment
which had not yet arrived. A few trees formed a barricade at
the bridge, which was defended by a party of archers and match-
lock men. The Carews, ever foremost, led their horses over the
fence, and after some hard fighting, in which Sir Gawen Carew
was shot through the arm, the road was cleared, Lord Russell
passed over, and the skirmish became general. The Cornish at
last giving way, discipline (as might be expected from such troops
as Russell had with him) gave way. They scattered looking for
spoil, and in this condition were caught by the second body of
insurgents, who came at the moment. They suffered severely,
many were cut to pieces, the rest extricated themselves after a
fierce struggle, rallied again, and finally drove the Cornish off
the field, leaving three hundred of their number dead; but
Russell's loss was probably as great as that of the rebels, and
he returned to Honiton in haste, not without fear of being inter-
cepted. . . . On Saturday, the 3rd of August, the little army
marched out of Honiton. To avoid a battle, where they could
not choose their ground, they left the road, crossed the open
hills [*Woodbury Common*] behind Ottery St. Mary, and in the
evening of the same day were on the heath—or what was a heath
in those days—above St. Mary's Clyst, two miles from Topsham."—
Froude's History of England, vol. v., pp. 189-191.

D

APPENDIX E.

Ottery St. Mary occupied by the Parliamentary Forces in 1645.

"On the 29th of October in this year, Fairfax sent away the train of artillery towards St. Mary Autree, and followed after himself, resolving to refresh his army, which never stood in more need of it, by laying them in the best and most convenient quarters he could. From Saturday, November 15th, to Tuesday, December 2nd, the general continued at Autree, riding about sometimes to see the finishing of the works at Broadclyste and Poultemore, and disposing of the quarters for the foot, who were sick in most places, there dying of soldiers and inhabitants of the town of Autree seven, eight, and nine a day, for several weeks together, insomuch that it was not held safe for the head quarters to be continued there any longer. Colonel Pickering, that pious, active gentleman that lived so much to God and his country, and divers other officers died of the new disease in that place. Six of the general's own family were sick of it at one time, and, throughout the foot regiments, half the soldiers. Yet, notwithstanding, at this very time did the army undergo very hard censures by some for not being in action. . . . Yet a few days the general continued at Autree, but resolved forthwith to remove (in regard the disease increased so fast) to Tiverton, which place was agreed on to be a head quarter, which resolution was actuated on Saturday."—*From Sprigge's " England's Recovery,"* p. 155.

Oliver Cromwell in Ottery St. Mary, 1645.

"About the time that Exeter was besieged, Cromwell came to Ottery St. Mary to raise men and money from the town and neighbourhood. For this purpose he held a convention there in a parlour, now standing westward of the Church, in one of the old Collegiate houses just without the boundaries of the Church-yard." [*This parlour was destroyed some years since in the course of alterations of the house in question, now called " Heath's Court," but originally, " The Chantry."*] " The people of Ottery," Polwhele continues, "refused to comply with his requisition. There is a remonstrance against his unjust demand now existing in a chest belonging to the Corporation of Ottery St. Mary, signed by the principal inhabitants of the parish ; and Cromwell was so irritated that he ordered his men to destroy all the ornaments of the Church, &c., &c." By the courtesy of the governors, search has been made among their papers, but the document in question cannot be found. In the course of the search, however, the following letter was discovered (in reference to some petition to His Highness the Lord Protector), which is worth insertion here :

" Gentlemen and my much honored freinds

   Yours of ffebruarie last I had answered before this had any thing by our actinge beene produced considerable, but truly as the woorke is great soe it hath greatly troubled vs, to bring it to that pointe, on which it now standeth.—

 Yesterday hauuing receaued our Petition with his Hignesse order indorse and directed to the Gouernors of the rents and profitts of Windsor Castle, for to consider of and returne theere answer how our inst desires mentioned in the said petition may bee effected : I carried the same Petition soe indorsed and did deliuer it to Mr Crescet one of the said Gouernors who did professe to mee that the said Petition was very conscionable and that att the next meeting of the said Gouernors (wch will bee sometime betwixt this and the five twenteth of this month) hee will labor to the vttermost of his power for a compleat and satisfactorie answer, but withall telling mee that though the mowes should bee setled for the payment of 200^{li} ℞ ann. yet hee feared that wee should receaue but small proffitt att the present, till moore of theese Rents shall fall into hand, & his reason was because his Hignesse had granted, above two yeares since 200^{li} ℞ ann : to the Tryers* & Approuers of Minnisters att White-Hall which they neuer receaued before this yeare. ffor the curing of this euill (if it shall befall vs) I would aduise you to speake with Mr. Bamfeild, who promised mee by the helpe of his friends to procure a competent Augmentation fro the Trustees till our sheaues or mowes shall fall into hand. I suppose it will not bee necessarie for mee to attend this businesse any longer, for I am persuaded that your Agent Mr. Light with my cosen Maydstone his helpe and assistance will bee able, it being soe farr on foote, to runn it downe & to bring it to good effect. howeuer I am resolued att present not to mooue without youre order, the wch I desier to vnderstand by the next Post.

 Concerning the fitt man that you desired mee in the said letter to finde for you : I have thus farr proceeded therein. I first spake with Mr. Calame & then with Dr. Reynolds, who promised to assist mee to the best of his power, & for that end granted mee his letter to Dr. Connant Rect^{r.} of Exon Colledg in Oxford, for to procure vs a learned & pious man, who presenting himselfe & preaching vnto you if you & the parish shall approoue of him you may elect him, according to the power granted vnto you, if not you are to bee pleased to giue him his charges and hee is to returne againe. But this day I haue receaued another letter fro you intimating other resolutions ; what to doe how I may come off ciuilly & with flying colours, having soe farr proceeded I must leaue to your better iudgments desiring by the next Post to vnderstand your pleasures therein. I haue not moore of import to add, but to desier of God to give good successe to yovr good desires & indeauors. Subscribing myselfe

Yovr truly louing neighbor & servant

London this 14th of March :   FRAN : YOUNG.
    1657.

[Addressed]   To the wor^{ll.} Gideon Haydoⁿ
            Esq., Rich : Channon esq.,
            & the rest of the Gouern^{rs}
            & Assistants of the
            Parishe of Otterie
            St. Mary present this
               neere
                 Hoineton.
        Leave this with Mr. Palfrey,
          in Otterie aforesaid.
        Post is paid.
            (Deuon.)

It does not appear whether the Minister in question was intended to fill any recognised office in the Parish Church, or to officiate as a lecturer, which many were apt to do about this time, without either

---

* In 1653-4 an Act passed which required all persons who were presented to any Benefice or Lecture to be examined by a Committee of Tryers, from whom, if approved, they received an instrument equivalent to Letters of Institution or Induction.

consulting the Ordinary, or observing the Canons and discipline of the Church. It is on record that "the Rev. Richard Newte, Rector of Tidcombe Portion, Tiverton, was expelled from his Rectory by the Tryers, and went afterwards to Ottery St. Mary, and preached a lecture on Wednesdays (on a salary of £20 per annum), but from this lectureship he was expelled at the end of a year."

Another document, among the Corporation Papers, was a Dispensation from the Lenten Fast, issued by Archbishop Juxon in 1662. It is written in Latin, and follows a form not uncommon in those days. It is signed at the foot: *Wmus. Sherman Regrius.*

APPENDIX F.

Execution of Rebels after the Battle of Sedgemoor.

We have seen how the parish of Ottery was, as it were, on the edge of the storm during the Cornish insurrection in 1549; and how, after the lapse of another century, it had bitter experience of a hostile occupation by the troops of parliament (1645). Forty years later, an incident occurred, exhibiting in a striking manner, the fearful consequences of an insurrection. The Duke of Monmouth landed at Lyme on the 11th of June, 1685, with about 100 followers, and within four days multitudes flocked to his standard to the number of 2000 horse and foot, from all quarters. At this time, Escot House was in course of erection by Sir Walter Yonge, and several of the workmen employed in the building left their work and joined the insurgents. The battle of Sedgemoor was fought on Sunday, the 16th of July; and these men being taken prisoners were ordered by Judge Jeffries to be brought down and hung at a four cross-road at Talewater (known ever since by the sad name of Bittery Cross), about a mile from Escot House, as a warning to the neighbours. It is supposed that the selection of this spot for the execution was intended as a "personal or rather political affront" to Sir Walter Yonge, who had entertained the Duke of Monmouth in his famous progress through the western counties five years before, and had thus been brought undeservedly under the suspicions of the Government. One of our oldest inhabitants states that his mother (who lived to an advanced age) remembered the stumps of some posts at Spence Cross (where the Station Road crosses the London Road) which were said to have served for gibbets after a public execution, and it is not unlikely that the bodies of some of those, who suffered on this occasion, were suspended there for the sake of greater publicity.

APPENDIX G.

Antient Ecclesiastical Districts, &c., within the Parish.

The town appears to have been antiently divided into three districts, designated as Ottery St. Mary, Ottery St Saviour, and Ottery St. Budeaux. The Chapel of St. Saviour was near the bridge of the same name, and it appears from Bishop Grandisson's Register (June 1, 1355) that he had recently erected it. Bishop Lacy granted an indulgence of 40 days for the repairs of the said Chapel and bridge in 1438; and in 1531, Bishop Veysey permitted one Selman to become a recluse in it. A block of buildings which contained portions of carved stone, and went by the name of St. Budeaux, was consumed by fire not many years ago. It stood to the east of Sherman's almshouses, on the opposite side of Jesu street. There were also domestic Chapels or Oratories attached to the mansion houses at Knightstone and Holcombe (the latter dedicated to St. Leonard), erected under licences from Bishop Brantyngham in the years 1381 and 1388.

APPENDIX H.

The Sherman and Hone Almshouses.

"Neat, but void of state,
"Where age and want sit smiling at the gate."

The almshouses in *Jesu* (otherwise *Yonder*) *street* are said to have been founded by the Sherman family, who settled at Knightstone about the year 1547. At the eastern gable there was a small Chapel for the use of the inmates, rising to the whole height of the roof, and abutting upon the road which is still called *Chip* (an abbreviation for *Chapel*) *lane*. The premises being very dilapidated were rebuilt by the Feoffees of the Ottery charities in 1837, and are now capable of accommodating twenty-four inmates, who are maintained by weekly allowance from the funds of the trust.

The almshouses in *Sandhill* (anciently *Sandye*) *street* were built by Robert Hone, Esq., one of whose daughters and coheiresses, Joan, married John Bodley, of Exeter, and was the mother of Sir Thomas Bodley, founder of the Bodleian library. The houses are occupied by nine aged or infirm women who are maintained from the funds of the Feoffee charities.

APPENDIX I.

Fires in Ottery St. Mary.

This parish cannot compete with Crediton or Tiverton for the "painful pre-eminence in conflagrations;" but there are records of three extensive fires within the last three centuries. A memorandum on the fly-leaf of the earliest register states that the first occurred in "Julye, Ano. Dni. 1604, when the lower part of the towne of Ottery St. Marye was consumed with fire." In the Minutes of the Magistrates at the Castle of Exeter on 10th of July, 1604, collections were ordered for the relief of the sufferers; and, probably in pursuance of this order, there is an entry in the parish book of Heavitree, "Delivered unto Wm. Leigh, the constable of the parish, in August, 1604, towards the relieving of such as had taken great loss by misfortune of fire at Otterye, xvis. *(Communicated by Dr. Oliver in* 1832.)

"The Great Fire," as it was formerly called, took place on the 16th day of March, 1767, "by which" (according to a notice in the *Gentleman's Magazine*), "the best part of the town is said to be consumed." By that catastrophe (we learn from another source), fifty houses in the middle of the town were consumed, together with the market house, which then adjoined the premises of the King's School, the progress of the fire being stopped by the eastern gable of the schoolroom. A tradition prevailed fifty years ago as to the cause of the fire, viz.: that the fire engine was being exercised near the market place, and some beggars, who were passing by at the time, were fiercely played upon by the fire men. Whereupon, one of them turned round and threatened that the Ottery people should soon have some other work for their engine; and the fire which broke out on the following day was, not unreasonably, attributed to their desire of vengeance.

Both these visitations, however, were eclipsed by the fire which commenced at noon on the 25th day of May, 1866, and in the space of four hours destroyed 111 houses, and rendered 500 persons houseless. It broke out in a cottage adjoining the National School premises in Jesu street, quickly ran along the eaves of the thatched roof of the school, and leaping over many blocks of houses in its capricious course, came at length within a dangerous proximity to the corn mills and silk factory. It had been preceded by a long drought, and was followed on the next day by a profuse downfall of rain. The benevolence of the public was equal to this great emergency. Scarcely had twelve days passed from the issue of a simple appeal for help, before the munificent sum of no less than £3530 was subscribed, in addition to a bountiful supply of wearing apparel, and other necessaries for distribution among the most necessitous; and the subscription list was closed. By God's mercy, no one sustained any personal injury on that eventful day; but it is sad to relate, that on Sunday, the 2nd of September following, a chimney, which had been suffered to remain standing among the ruins, fell across the street, where a crowd of people were assembled to listen to the preaching of a woman from Exeter, whereby eight persons were killed, and fourteen others severely injured. Six out of the eight happily were unmarried, and the other two, a man and his wife, were childless, so that none of the survivors had to lament the loss of a parent or a partner.

APPENDIX J.

Traces of Pestilence in former times.

1.

The Register of Burials shows that there was a great mortality in the parish in the months July—November, 1604, probably from an outbreak of the plague which raged in Exeter towards the close of the previous year, and was carrying off 3,000 a week in London during this year.

2.

Again, in 1621 the Burials far exceeded the usual average; and it is recorded that Exeter was again suffering from pestilence in this year.

3.

Again, in 1645 (immediately on the evacuation of the town by the Parliamentary troops) there ensued a great mortality among the inhabitants; and whereas the number of burials usually averaged 42 per annum, 81 were interred in the month of December, and 37 in the first fifteen days of January, when the entries are abruptly broken off, and there is a blank for many months following.

4.

Again, in the last six months of 1741 the interments are increased four-fold; and it is recorded that, at this same date, one-twelfth part of the population of Tiverton was carried off by an epidemic disease, which was called "the spotted fever."

5.

Within the memory of the present generation, in spite of great natural advantages of position and climate, and abundance of water, the town was frequently visited with epidemic disorders, owing, in a great degree, to the want of sanitary precautions. A return made to the Central Board of Health from the Honiton Union (1st February, 1849), reported that "the parish of Ottery St. Mary appears to be the only one where there is a prevalence of disease in this neighbourhood, 71 *cases of fever having occurred between the latter end of August and the third week in October!*" This state of things led to the establishment of the Local Board of Health in the following year (July, 1850), and since it came into full operation, it is not too much to say that the sanitary condition of the parish has been unimpeachable. It should be a matter of great thankfulness to be able to record that it was never visited with the Asiatic cholera.

APPENDIX K.

Population, Rental, and Rating of the Parish.

It is very difficult to arrive at any precise information touching our population in earlier times; but it appears that it has not kept pace with the general rate of increase throughout the kingdom, our numbers having only increased fifty per cent. during the 110 years preceding the census of 1801. There is still extant a rate made on the 26th day of May, Anno Domini 1690, "for raising money by a poll or otherwise towards the reducing of Ireland, and prosecuting the war against France" *(Anno Secundo Gul. iii. and M.)* The enumeration of persons on the poll gives a population of 1632; and the assessment amounted to £128 12s. 8d. The names of all persons, except the apprentices, are given at length, and it is worthy of notice, that only one person on the roll has a second Christian name.

The decennial returns of the Census during the present century have been as follows:

1801	..	..	2415	1841	..	..	4194
1811	..	..	2880	1851	..	..	4421
1821	..	..	3522	1861	..	..	4340
1831	..	..	3849				

In 1861 the males amounted to 2043, and the females to 2297. The inhabited houses 925; uninhabited, 34; building, 6: of these, the town district contained 536 inhabited houses, and a population of 2534. The gross estimated rental of the parish, according to the last returns to the Poor Law Board (1865) amounted to £19,345. The rate per pound to the relief of the poor on gross estimated rental for the year ending Lady Day, 1864 (*i.e.*, before the Union Chargeability Act came into operation), was 1s. 7¼d.

APPENDIX L.

Longevity of the Inhabitants.

Polwhele (vol. i., p. 327) writes, "Very few of the inhabitants of Ottery St. Mary exceed the age of 90, though many live to that age. Mrs. Heath, who lived in Oliver Cromwell's Convention House, died the latter end of June, 1786, aged 113. She retained her faculties to the last; she had the clearest recollection of the principal occurrences in her own family, and perfectly remembered a number of distant events, both public and private, among which was the landing of King William at Torbay, with a great variety

ticulars relating to that circumstance." In the early Burial
ers of the parish the age is very rarely inserted except on
rdinary occasions; but the following entries occur of the
ent of centenarians :

    1749 John Wall, a pauper, said to be 110.
    1754 Elizabeth Woodford, widow, aged 100.
    1824 Sarah Eveleigh, 101.

ater Registers show that the parish still supports its reputation
ngevity. Between the years 1851 and 1867 the burials are
led of the following individuals, distinguished here by their
s and sex :

		Sex	Age	Year			Sex	Age
..	J. B. ..	(F.)	.. 98	1861	.. E. D. ..	(F.)	.. 90
..	W. M. ..	(M.)	.. 91	1862	.. M. B. ..	(F.)	.. 92
..	T. G ..	(M.)	.. 91	——	.. M. C. ..	(F.)	.. 91
..	M. W. ..	(F.)	.. 93	——	.. M. G. ..	(F.)	.. 93
..	J. S. ..	(M.)	.. 90	——	.. H. B. ..	(F.)	.. 92
..	R. S. ..	(M.)	.. 92	1863	.. G. D. ..	(M.)	.. 94
..	S. P. ..	(F.)	.. 97	——	.. C. M. ..	(F.)	.. 91
..	E. S. ..	(F.)	.. 90	1864	.. B. C. ..	(F.)	.. 90
..	H. W. ..	(F.)	.. 98	1867	.. B. R. ..	(M.)	.. 90
..	A. H. ..	(F.)	.. 90	——	.. M. M. ..	(F.)	.. 92
..	G. K. ..	(M.)	.. 90				

ll be seen that the proportion of females to males is as two to

341 interments in the parish Churchyard, between 19th
ary, 1851, and 11th April, 1857,

    114 had passed their sixtieth,
     83   ,,   ,,   seventieth,
     35   ,,   ,,   eightieth, and
      9   ,,   ,,   ninetieth year.

APPENDIX M.

Biographical Notices of Deceased Persons connected with the Parish of Ottery St. Mary.

JOHN DE GRANDISSON, Bishop of Exeter, the munificent founder
. Mary's College, Ottery, was the second son of Lord William
randisson, who was summoned to Parliament among the Barons
e realm in the reign of Edward I. The family was among
most noble in the Palatinate of Burgundy, and connected with
Emperor of Constantinople, the King of Hungary, and the
es of Bavaria. Lord William is said to have accompanied
and, Earl of Lancaster, brother of King Edward I. into
and, where he married Sibilla de Tregoz, the wealthy heiress
ohn, Lord Tregoz, of Ewias, in Herefordshire. The future
op was born at Ashton, in Herefordshire in 1292, and after

E

receiving Holy Orders, was collated to the Prebend of Haydore in Lincoln Cathedral, and subsequently to the Archdeaconry of Nottingham. Whilst Chaplain to Pope John XXII., he was joined in a commission to negociate the peace of Gascony, when the news reached the Papal court at Avignon, of the premature death of James de Berkley, Bishop of Exeter (1327), whereupon His Holiness immediately appointed him to the vacant See, and the ceremony of consecration was performed by Peter, Cardinal Bishop of Præneste (whose obit was ordered to be kept in our Collegiate Church on 17th of May), on Sunday, the 18th day of October, in the Dominican Church of Avignon. He succeeded to the peerage on the death of his brother Peter, Lord Grandisson, in 1358, and died on the 15th of July, 1369, in the 77th year of his age, and the 42nd of his consecration. For an account of his episcopate, and the munificence of his ecclesiastical endowments, the reader must be referred to Dr. Oliver's *Monasticon* and *Lives of the Bishops of Exeter*. Mr. Edward Smirke notes his benevolent act of abolishing all personal servitude in the manor of Ottery, and allowing the redemption of marriage fines in consideration of a fixed yearly rent of 2*s*. 6*d*. a ferling, "pro licentia maritandi filias suas, &c., et pro operibus hyemalibus et autumpnalibus, &c., et consuetudinibus exonerandis" (except suit to mill, heriots, &c.) Hooker writing in 1599 states that "his tombe (in the Chapel of St. Radegundes, in Exeter Cathedral) was of late pulled up, the ashes scattered abroad, and the bones bestowed no man knoweth where." "Surely (adds Izacke in his *Memorials)* the reliques of this worthy prelate deserved a more reverent respect even among savage beasts."

2. WILLIAM BROWNE was born at Tavistock in 1588, and pursued his studies at Exeter College, Oxford, until he removed without taking a degree to the Inner Temple, where, we are told, he more particularly devoted himself to the Muses. The degree of M.A. was conferred on him in 1624, and he shortly after was received into the family of William, Earl of Pembroke. Wood in his *Athenæ Oxonienses* is very doubtful with regard to his death, for all that he says of the matter is, that in his searches he finds one William Browne, of Ottery St. Mary, died in the year 1645, but that he cannot tell whether he was the same with our poet. It is tolerably certain that nothing is heard of him after that date, and it does not appear that any other locality claims to be the place of his interment. Southey, the late Poet Laureate, when visiting the Church, expressed his opinion that the beautiful epitaphs in St. Stephen's Chapel, commencing with "If wealth, wit, beauty," and "Under this monument, &c.," were written by Browne, which would be strong presumptive evidence of his connection with the parish. His principal works are *The Shepherd's Pipe* and *Britannia's Pastorals*, and critics are of opinion that Milton borrowed the idea of Comus from Browne's *Inner Temple Masque*, and that Lycidas owes its origin to *Philarete* (*Vide* Fourth Eclogue.)

3. **The Rev. Melchizedeck Alford** was a student of Christ Church, from which he was expelled during the Great Rebellion. "Afterwards he became Treasurer to the garrison of Exeter, when it was besieged by the rebels (1646), and was employed in carrying letters and other messages to the king at Oxford and elsewhere. He assisted also in carrying off the Duke of Gloucester; but being never rewarded for his services after the Restoration, he died (1689), possessed of no greater preferment than the poor Vicaridge of Autery in Devon." He married Elizabeth, only daughter and heiress of Richard Channon, the owner of Escot, and in 1680 joined with his wife and two daughters in conveying Escot to Sir Walter Yonge. His wife survived him many years, and her memory is preserved in the remarkable will of Mr. Axe, who directed that a certain proportion of the income of his charitable bequests to the parish of Ottery should be applied for the benefit of the sick and aged, "to some man or woman of exemplary life, and indifferent skill in physic and surgery, if they shall be very fit, or as fit as Mrs. Alford, the late Vicar's wife, who delighted in such things." Melchizedeck Alford is said to have been a true loyalist, a man of very bright and excellent parts, and the author of those well-known lines, which he is said to have made extempore in a company who were criticizing the inscription that was set up over the gates of the Louvre, beginning with "Non orbis gentem, &c."

> Louvra domus; Dominus Ludovicus: Regia Rege
> Digna suo. Cælo est hæc minor, ille Deo!

4. **Thomas Axe**, a liberal and judicious benefactor to Ottery St. Mary, was the eldest son of George Axe, the parish clerk, and born in December, 1635. Nothing is known of his early history, but it appears from his will that he married a daughter of Dr. Bristall, master of the King's School, who had formerly been master of the school at Blandford. It was probably through the interest of his father-in-law that he was employed as assistant steward in the management of the estates of Sir William Portman, Bart., of Bryantstone, near Blandford, under Mr. Colby; and on his decease he became sole steward of the property, and removed to Orchard Portman. Lord Portman (to whose courtesy I am indebted for this information) states that the property of Southwark, of which Mr. Axe died possessed, was mixed up with that of some of his family. He left a widow and one child, for whose "educating and bringing up to some good honest way of living," he directs his trustees (one of whom was Mr. Keeble, bookseller of St. Dunstan's parish in the West, London) to apply a moiety of his rents. We may judge of the respect in which he was held by his employers from the circumstance that he leaves "mourning rings to his honoured friends Sir John Cutler, Henry Portman, Esq., Henry Wallop, Esq., and Mrs. Mary Stonehouse, who have been godfathers and godmother to my children;" and also to Mrs. Phillippa Speke, Captain Humphry Coles, and Mrs. Claudia St. John, who were connected with the Portman family. The disposition of his property, upon the death of his son without issue, is set forth in the tablet

enumerating his bequests, erected . in the south porch by the Governors, whom he constituted his trustees. One remarkable feature in his will was, a bequest of one thousand pounds to any person who should discover a ready and easy way to find the true longitude at sea, within ten years of his decease. As this was not claimed, it fell into the estate devoted to charitable uses. Mr. Axe was buried at Orchard Portman, near Taunton, August 1st, 1691, but "never marked the marble with his name."

5. John Coleridge was born in the year 1718 ; and on 13th of June, 1749, was elected master of Squire's Endowed "Latin School," at Southmolton. He was ordained Deacon (24th September, 1749) and Priest (23rd December, 1750) by Bishop Lavington, in the Chapel of the Virgin Mary, in the Palace, Exeter, on the Curacy of Mariansleigh as his title ;. and licensed to the Lectureship at Molland ·in 1753. On the death of the Rev. Richard Holmes, he was elected Chaplain Priest and Master of the King's School on the 20th of August, 1760, and was presented to the Vicarage of Ottery St. Mary on the 27th of December following. He is said to have been a man of great learning, and to have assisted Dr. Kennicott in the publication of his famous edition of the Hebrew Bible. Besides his contributions to the *Gentleman's Magazine*, on Classical and Biblical Criticism, he published the following works :
1. *A short Grammar on the Latin Tongue*, 1759.
2. *Miscellaneous Dissertations on the xvii. and xviii. chapters of Judges*, 1768.
3. *A Critical Latin Grammar, with notes for youths somewhat advanced in Latin learning*, 1772.
4. *Government, not originally proceeding from human agency, but from Divine institution: a Fast Sermon on the breaking out of the American War, preached at Ottery, December 13th*, 1776.
He was "an exceedingly studious man, pious, of primitive manners, and of the most simple habits; passing events were little heeded by him, and therefore he was usually characterized as the ' absent man.' " (*Gillman's Life of S. T. Coleridge.*) His sermons are said to have been very attractive to the agricultural population, from the circumstance of his frequently quoting the Scriptures in the original Hebrew, which he usually prefaced by saying that he would give them the very language of the Holy Ghost. He died suddenly, in the sixty-third year of his age, on the 14th of October, 1781.

6. Sir Francis Buller was born 17th March, 1746, and is said to have accompanied the Rev. John Coleridge to Ottery, when he exchanged Southmolton School for the King's School, 1760. Three years later we find him, while yet "in statu pupillari," married in the Parish Church by license to Miss Susannah Yarde, whose family resided at the Warden House. He immediately entered at the Temple; and the responsibilities of a husband at seventeen, and of a parent at twenty gave such an impetus to his industry, that he very soon took up a conspicious position at the Bar, and was almost as precocious in his preferment as he had been in his

marriage, being appointed a Puisne Judge in the King's Bench at the early age of thirty-two (1778) on the earnest recommendation of the Chief Justice, Lord Mansfield. So highly did he esteem him that ten years later he endeavoured to induce Mr. Pitt to consent to his being appointed his successor, and to that end delayed for a time his own resignation. The minister, however, declined to accede to the proposal, and gave him instead what was regarded as the "very inadequate compensation of a baronetcy" in January, 1790. Sir Francis Buller died 5th June, 1800, aged fifty-four. His only son assumed the additional surname of Yarde, upon succeeding to a large property through his mother; and his grandson was raised to the peerage as Baron Churston, in 1858. Mr. Foss (from whose *Judges of England*, vol. viii., p. 251, many of the preceding facts are derived) says that "Sir Francis Buller is equally celebrated among both females and males, but not with equal admiration. While he is considered by the latter as one of the most learned of the lawyers, he is stigmatized by the former as one of the most cruel of judges, since to him is attributed the obnoxious and ungentlemanly dictum, that a husband may beat his wife, so that the stick with which he administers the castigation is not thicker than his thumb. It may, perhaps, restore him to the ladies' good graces to be told, that though the story was generally believed, and even made the subject of a caricature, yet after a searching investigation by the most able critics and antiquaries, no substantial evidence can be found that he ever expressed so ungallant an opinion."

7. SIR ISAAC HEARD, Knight, Garter Principal King of Arms, was born at Ottery St. Mary, 10th December, 1730, Old Style, and died 22 April, 1822, in the ninety-second year of his age. In early life he entered the Navy as a midshipman, but quitted the service in 1751, and eight years after was appointed by the Earl of Effingham, then exercising the office of Earl Marshal for the Duke of Norfolk, to the office of Blue Mantle Pursuivant of Arms. He rose by degrees to the highest dignity in the Herald's College, and proclaimed George IV. on the 31st January, 1820, but was unable to take part in his Coronation. It is a curious fact that he officiated at the interment of a Prince or Princess of each generation in a succession of six generations of the House of Brunswick, beginning with King George II., and ending with the Princess Charlotte and her Royal Infant. While serving as a midshipman on board the *Blandford*, off the coast of Guinea (1750), he was carried overboard from the effect of a tornado, with the mainmast of the ship, whilst standing on the topsail yard, encouraging the sailors to their duty. By the interposition of Providence, at a moment when the attention of the whole crew was directed to disencumber the vessel from the wreck, he was observed enveloped in the shattered rigging, floating alongside of the ship, and he owed his immediate rescue to the hand of his shipmate, afterwards Admiral Sir Robert Kingsmill. In grateful commemoration of his wonderful escape from death, he adopted the following arms, which were assigned to him when he

became Lancaster Herald: *Argent,* a Neptune crowned with an eastern crown of gold, his trident *sable,* headed *or;* issuing from a stormy ocean, the sinister hand grasping the head of a ship's mast, appearing above the waves as part of the wreck, all proper on a chief *azure;* the Arctic Polar star of the first, between two water bougets of the second. His motto was: "Naufragus in portum." Sir Isaac Heard is said to have been an excellent Latin scholar, and a good modern linguist, which enabled him to acquit himself with great distinction on several occasions of the investiture of foreign princes.

8. SAMUEL TAYLOR COLERIDGE, the author of *Christabel,* &c., was the thirteenth child of the Rev. John Coleridge, Vicar and Chaplain Priest of Ottery St. Mary, and master of the King's School. He was born at the School House, October 21st, 1772, "about eleven o'clock in the forenoon," and had the misfortune to lose his father when he was but nine years of age. Through the interest of his father's celebrated pupil Sir Francis Buller, he obtained a nomination to Christ's Hospital, (then presided over by the Rev. James Bowyer), where he was the friend and contemporary of Charles Lamb (Elia), and Thomas Fanshawe Middleton, afterwards Bishop of Calcutta.. From Christ's Hospital he removed to Jesus College, Cambridge, and distinguished himself as an undergraduate, competing, "non sine gloria," with Keate, Butler, and Bethell. He left Cambridge without a degree, and henceforth adopted literature as a profession. His subsequent career is a part of the literary history of the country, and cannot be included in our narrow limits. It may suffice to quote Wordsworth's opinion of his powers, that "many men of his age had done wonderful *things,* as Davy, Scott, Cuvier, &c., but that Coleridge was the only wonderful *man* he ever knew." He died at Highgate, 26th July, 1834. Considering the clearness of his intellectual powers, and the phases of belief through which he passed in his pursuit of the truth, it is a comfort to read the following earnest confession of his faith, as expressed in his last will and testament (dated 17th September, 1829), "I hope to rise, through the merits and mediation, and by the efficacious power of the Son of God, Incarnate in the Blessed Jesus, Whom, I believe in my heart, and confess with my mouth, to have been from everlasting the Way and the Truth, and to have become Man, that for fallen and sinful men He might be the Resurrection and the Life."

9. RICHARD HURRELL FROUDE, eldest son of Archdeacon Froude, was born 25th March, 1803, and died at Dartington, 28th February, 1836. After receiving the earlier part of his education at the King's School, he went to Eton in 1816, and thence to Oriel College, Oxford, where he was elected Fellow in 1826. He contributed to the *Tracts for the Times* and the *British Critic,* and was the author of eight poems in the *Lyra Apostolica,* distinguished by the letter Beta. Dr. Newman published his *Remains* in 4 vols., in 1838-9. "Froude was a man of rare ability."—(*Quarterly Review,* No. ccliii., p. 120.)

10. HENRY NELSON COLERIDGE, fourth son of Colonel James Coleridge, was born at Heath's Court, in the parish of Ottery St. Mary, 25th October, 1798. From the King's School he went to Eton College, where he gave great promise of future distinction in literature, by his contributions to *The Etonian*, usually under the initials G. M. (Gerard Montgomery,) which was the character which he sustained among the members of The King of Clubs. In 1823, he became fellow of King's College, Cambridge, where he was Browne's medallist for Latin and Greek Odes; and was called to the Bar by the Hon. Society of the Middle Temple in 1826. He practised as an Equity Draftsman and Conveyancer, and was appointed Lecturer on the Principles and Practice of Equity to the Incorporated Law Society. He published *Six Months in the West Indies*, and *Introduction to the Study of the Greek Classic Poets*, contributed occasionally articles to the *Quarterly Review*, and edited *The Literary Remains of Samuel Taylor Coleridge*, his uncle and father-in-law. He died 26th January, 1843. His friend and contemporary Winthrop Mackworth Praed (the Peregrine Courtenay of the *Etonian*), inherited the estate of Hayne, in Ottery St. Mary, but was not connected with the parish by birth or education.

11. GEORGE JAMES CORNISH, eldest son of George Cornish, Esq., of Salcombe House, Sidmouth, and Sarah his wife (of the family of the Kestells of Egloshayle, in the county of Cornwall) was born at the Manor House, Ottery St. Mary, 7th June, 1794, and educated at the King's School until he was of an age to be removed to Westminster. Thence he was elected Scholar of Corpus Christi College, Oxford (where he contracted a life-long friendship with Keble), and obtained a place in the first-class in Literis Humanioribus in 1813. In 1828 he was appointed Chaplain by Bishop Carey, formerly Head Master of Westminster School, and collated to the important vicarage of Kenwyn and Kea, near Truro. Bishop Phillpotts subsequently appointed him Prebendary of Exeter Cathedral. He died 10th September, 1849. A posthumous volume of his Sermons and Poetical Remains was published some years ago; and those who are acquainted with his beautiful Poems entitled *Egloshayle*, and *The Vale of Otter*, in *Days and Seasons, or Church Poetry for the Year*, will be glad to hear that there is hope of another volume of his Poems being published. He was singularly retiring in his disposition and character, but he was highly appreciated by his intimate friends, and his memory is enshrined in the hearts of all that knew and loved him. No apology is necessary for inserting the following lines, in consideration of their association with the dearly loved place of his birth.

The Vale of Otter.

O Sal'ston knoll! I love you well,
    And all your beechen skreen,
And yon east hill's continuous swell,
    And Otter's brook between;
Your breeze, your waters, and your shade,
Such as it is my Being made.

I love you well, sweet Vale! for here
  My stream of life arose;
That stream that through eternal years
  Shall flow as now it flows;
And howsoe'er it flows, from you
Borrows a still unchanging hue.

'Tis true; I know not what shall be
  When, all its wanderings ceased,
It joins at length its parent sea;
  But this I know at least,
He who a proper being gave,
That proper being still will save.

And, therefore, if some thoughts of blame
  And sorrow round thee cling,
Yet still, sweet Vale! I love thy name;
  Thou art a sacred thing;
Alike for evil and for good,
I cannot quit thee if I would.

Then honour to St. Mary's tower!
  The College and the School!
And honour to the Pixie's Bower!
  And to the Maiden Pool!
May they to boys hereafter be
The teachers they have been to me!

Still may these haunts, these groves, this sky,
  Kind ministrations yield!
The " common things that round them lie,"
  Their better nature build!
And teach them gently to improve
All harsher feelings into love.   C.

12. WILLIAM HART COLERIDGE, was the only child of Luke Herman Coleridge (the seventh son of the Rev. John Coleridge) and born at Thorverton on the 27th June, 1789. He lost his father in his infancy, and was brought up by his uncle, the Rev. George Coleridge, at the King's School, until he entered at Christ Church, Oxford, where he was nominated to a Studentship in 1811. His name appeared in the same year in the first class both in classics and mathematics. After officiating for several years as Assistant Curate of St. Andrews, Holborn, he was recommended by his Diocesan for the newly constituted See of Barbadoes and the Leeward Islands, and received Consecration in 1824. The important events of his Episcopate extending over nearly eighteen years (during which the Emancipation Act was carried into full effect) cannot be chronicled here; and it must suffice to state that when the Bishop felt himself unequal any longer to resist the influences of a tropical climate, he resigned his important charge, which was thenceforward divided into three Dioceses. After six years of comparative retirement in Ottery St. Mary, he was summoned by the Archbishop to accept the Wardenship of St. Augustine's College, Canterbury. This post, for which he was preeminently qualified, he held for the short space of fourteen months, when, after having been privileged to inaugurate a great work for the Church of Christ in either hemisphere, it pleased God in His great mercy to call him to his reward suddenly, by " a gentle wafting to eternal life," on St. Thomas' Day, 1849.

13. JAMES PULMAN was born at Ottery St. Mary in the year 1783, and early entered the Herald's College under the auspices of his friend Sir Isaac Heard, who was greatly attached to him. He was appointed Portcullis in 1822; Richmond Herald in 1837; Norroy King of Arms in 1847; and Clarencieux King of Arms in 1848. He also held the office of Yeoman Usher of the Black Rod in the House of Lords, the duties of which he discharged with great grace and dignity. Mr. Pulman was a man of extensive reading, far beyond the limited range of his professional studies, and ever ready to assist students in their researches, especially in all matters of antiquarian interest. Although thus profuse in the communication of his information and well-digested knowledge, he is not known to have published anything in his own name, but contributed freely from his stores to the elucidation of the history and antiquities of his native county. He died on the 29th October, 1859, in the 76th year of his age.

14. SIR GEORGE CORNISH WHITLOCK, K.C.B., the eldest son of George Whitlock, Esq., was born at Ottery St. Mary, 3rd December, 1798. He entered the military service in the East Indian Company in 1818, and was attached to the Madras Presidency, in which he served with great distinction. In 1845, he was appointed Lieutenant-Colonel of the Madras European regiment, and in April, 1858, he captured Banda from the rebels, the force under his command acting in conjunction with General Sir Hugh Rose (Lord Strathnairn.) He had previously, as Brigadier General of the 2nd Class, commanded at Bangalore. For his eminent services in Central India, he was made extra Knight Commander of the Order of the Bath, and appointed Colonel of the 108th Regiment. He died at Exmouth, January 30th, 1868.

APPENDIX N.

List of Vicars, Schoolmasters, and Chaplain Priests.

Vicars.

Ralph Mainwarynge..	..	1580	Hugh Lewes ..	.. 1713
Nicholas Forward ..	..	1590	Richard Jenkinson* ..	.. 1713
John Forward ..	..	1626	Ralph Farthing ..	.. 1722
Melchizedeck Alford..	..	1660	Richard Holme ..	.. 1743
William Hull ..	..	1691	John Coleridge, B.A. ..	.. 1760
John Rost	..	1692	Fulwood Smerdon, M.A.	.. 1781
—— Burrows ..	..	1694	George Smith, M.A. ..	.. 1794
Thomas Gatchell ..	..	1695	Sidney W. Cornish, D.D.	.. 1841

* He assisted the Rev. John Walker in compiling *The Sufferings of the Clergy.*

Schoolmasters.

Antony Saunders	..	..	—— Chilcott	..	1
Thomas Passemer	..	1598	Richard Holme, M.A.	..	1
Samuel Randoll, B.A.	..	1618	John Coleridge, B.A.	..	1
Richard Mercer, M.A.	..	1623	John Warren	..	1
John Barnes	..	1627	Fulwood Smerdon, M.A.	..	1
John Ball, M.A.	..	1636	George Coleridge, B.A.	..	1
William Bristall, M.A.	..	1651	John Warren, D.D.	..	1
John Crosse	..	1655	Sidney W. Cornish, D.D.	..	1
Greaves Austen, M.A.	..	1662	George Smith, M.A.	..	1
Richard Marker, B.A.	..	1699			

Chaplain Priests.

John Haycroft	..	1607	Richard Jenkinson, M.A.	..	1
—— Bradford	..	1611	Matthew Mundy, B.A.	..	1
John Fley, M.A.	..	1616	Richard Holme, M.A.	..	1
Edmond Ayshford, B.A.	..	1630	John Coleridge, B.A.	..	1
Roger Ware	..	1634	John Warren	..	1
Thomas Forward, B.A.	..	1634	Fulwood Smerdon, M.A.	..	1
Hugh Gundrie	..	1634	George Coleridge, B.A.	..	1
George Hall	..	1649	George Smith, M.A.	..	1
John Fayre, M.A.	..	1654	Frederick Salter, B.A.	..	1
William Read, M.A.	..	1660	Henry Thurston Thomson, B.A.		1
John Rost, M.A.	..	1664	James Thomas Boles, M.A.	..	1
John Rost, M.A.	..	1671	Richard Hillman Podmore, M.A.		1
Edward Whiteway, M.A.	..	1672	Frederick John Coleridge, M.A.		1
John Rost, M.A.	..	1675	Edward George Hunt, M.A.	..	1
John Ellis, B.A.	..	1680-1	George Smith, M.A.	..	1
Thomas Gatchell, B.A.	..	1689			

Ministers of the District Churches.

* St. John the Evangelist, Tipton.

George William Chamberlain, M.A.	..	1840	George Dowell, M.A.	..	1
			Augustus Archer Hunt, M.A.	..	1

* St. Philip and St. James the Less, Escot.

Philip William Douglas, M.A.	..	1840	James Furnival, M.A.	1
Francis Thomas Hill	..	1848		

* St. Michael the Archangel, West Hill.

James Thomas Boles, M.A.	..	1846	John Coventry, M.A.	1
Robert Henry Fortescue, M.A.	..	1848	Alexander Peter Turquand, M.A.	1
William Buckland Lott, M.A	..	1848		

St. James the Great, Alfington.

James Henry Coleridge, M.A.	..	1849	George Mason, M.A.‡	1
Henry Gardiner, M.A.	..	1852	Edward Eade, M.A.	1
John Coleridge Patteson, M.A.†		1853	Henry McIntosh Crichlow, M.A.	1

* These three Perpetual Curacies became Vicarages (12th November, 1868), unde recent Act of Parliament.

† Bishop of Melanesia.　　　　　‡ Archdeacon of Honololu.

APPENDIX O.

The King's New Grammar School of Saint Mary of Ottery
(Anno Regni 37 Hen. VIII.)

There is little known of the early history or fortune of the King's School from its foundation in 1545 until the year 1639, when there is an order on the Books of the Corporation to increase the stipend of Mr. John Ball " in regard that he hath been a means to increase the number of scholars more than formerly have been, which is for the general good of the parish, &c." The School seems to have attained its height of prosperity, in point of numbers, in 1662-1699, under the mastership of the Rev. Greaves Austen, M.A., Student of Christ Church, Oxford, "he having for many years together near 200 scholars under his care in the said school." His immediate successor is recorded to have " reduced this most flourishing School to be without even one scholar;" and he at length resigned his office upon being threatened with an appeal to the Lord Chancellor as visitor. The School prospered again under the Rev. Richard Holme, and the Rev. John Coleridge, but again experienced a decline under the two succeeding masters. The Rev. George Coleridge, in his evidence before the Charity Commissioners, October 8th, 1819, stated that "the School of late years [1781-1794], had only been formally kept up, there might be one or two scholars; when he came to the School, he found the premises in a ruinous state, and the schoolroom was used for keeping rabbits and poultry." From this disgraceful state of things, however, it rose steadily, under the careful teaching and strict discipline of the Rev. George Coleridge, to the first place among the schools of the diocese; and its credit was fully maintained under his pupil and successor, the Rev. Dr. Warren.

At a time, like the present, when the merits of such educational establishments are freely discussed, and their endowments are supposed to be in jeopardy, it may not be inopportune to measure the advantages conferred upon the town and neighbourhood by the number of pupils admitted into the King's School during a period of seventy years, which has amounted to 712, having been as follows :

1794—1808 ..	..	..	.. 150
1808—1824 ..	..	..	.. 188
1824—1863 ..	..	..	.. 374

Such a consideration may surely be regarded, in our case, as a strong plea in arrest of judgment.

The following are a few of the most distinguished pupils of the School in addition to those included in the " Short Biographical Notices " (Appendix M.)

JOHN LUXMOORE, D.D., successively Bishop of Bristol, Hereford, and St. Asaph.

Robert Hurrell Froude, m.a., Archdeacon of Totnes.

John Taylor Coleridge, p.c., formerly one of the Judges in the Queen's Bench.

Stephen Creyke, m.a., Archdeacon of York and Canon Residentiary.

George Hole, b.c.l., Prebendary of Exeter.

James Duke Coleridge, d.c.l., Prebendary of Exeter.

Joseph Loscombe Richards, d.d., Rector of Exeter College.

George May Coleridge, m.a., successively Prebendary of Wells and Exeter.

Charles Edward Kennaway, m.a., formerly Fellow of St. John's College, Cambridge, and Hon. Canon of Gloucester.

Robert Holberton, m.a., Archdeacon of Antigua (1843-1850.)

Sackville U. B. Lee, m.a., Canon Residentiary of Exeter.

John Coleridge Patteson, d.d., Bishop of Melanesia. ("Unto me, who am less than the least of all saints, is this grace given, that I should preach among the Gentiles the unsearchable riches of Christ."—*Ephesians* iii., 8.)

APPENDIX P.

The Church Bells, the Curfew, and the Chimes.

1.

There is a peal of six bells in the south Tower, not remarkable for their antiquity or size. The following Table shows the weight of each bell and the date of its casting:

No.			cwt.	qrs		Date of Casting
1	..	..	5	3	..	1670
2	..	..	6	0	..	1680
3	..	..	7	3	..	1652
4	..	..	10	0	..	1671
5	..	..	11	0	..	1790
6	..	..	17	2	..	1727 (F.)

The fourth bell bears two satirical medals, one of which represents a Pope and a King under one face, and the other a Cardinal and a Bishop. These medals are shown in the Rev. H. T. Ellacombe's interesting Paper on "The Church Bells of Devon," published by the Exeter Diocesan Architectural Society (Second Series, Vol. i., p. 277.)

2

The Curfew bell has been rung here from time immemorial, at eight o'clock p.m., from Michaelmas to Lady-day, with the exception of Sundays, and the intervening days between Christmas Eve and the

Feast of the Epiphany. The same custom prevails here as at Carfax, Oxford, of ringing the day of the month, after the bell has sounded the Curfew. It is usual also to toll a bell for a quarter of an hour at eight o'clock a.m., on all Sundays throughout the year.

3

There are two ancient chime-barrels in the south tower attached to the bells; one of which is worked by a winch-crank, and is used daily during the last quarter of an hour before the commencement of Divine Service a.m., and at all the Services on Sundays. The other barrel is pricked with three Psalm tunes, changeable at pleasure, and put in motion by the clock at the hours of four, eight, and twelve; but the machinery is out of gear, and, to the great regret of the parishioners, these chimes have not been heard for many years.

APPENDIX Q.

Post-Reformation Services in the Parish Church.

King Henry VIII., in his Letters Patent, provided for keeping up the Public Services of the Church, by injoining the Governors to maintain two Chaplain Priests as Assistants to the Vicar or Perpetual Preacher. The Corporation, however, was relieved from the maintenance of more than one, by a decree of the Court of Exchequer (40 Eliz., 1598), "as long as they shall think one to be sufficient." It is evident, from the Minutes of the Corporation, that, as late as 1625, there was Daily Service in the Church, the Morning Prayer at eight, and the Evening Prayer at "half-an-hour after two;" and there is no reason to suppose that these Services were discontinued until the Liturgy of the Church of England was abolished by Act of Parliament in 1644, when it was enacted, that "every person who should use, or cause to be used, the *Book of Common Prayer* in any Church or Chapel, or any other public place of Worship, or *in any private place or family*, within the kingdom of England, should forfeit for the first offence £5, for the second £10, and for the third should suffer one whole year's imprisonment without bail or main prize!" During the time of the Commonwealth there was a total suspension of our Liturgical Services, and the exact date of their resumption is not known; but Walker, in his *Sufferings of the Clergy*, relates that "the Rev. Richard Venne, [Vicar of Otterton, 1625-1662], was said to be the first person who read Common Prayer in the neighbouring Church of Ottery St. Mary after the happy return of His Majesty." It does not however appear that the week-day Services were resumed, with the exception of Morning Prayer on Wednesdays and Fridays. The re-establishment of the Daily Morning Prayer dates from the 15th of August, 1842; to which Daily Evening Prayer was added on the 15th of May, 1850. The weekly administration of the Holy Communion was commenced on the 5th March, 1843, and Congregational Baptisms on the 19th day of the same month and year. An immediate increase of 25 per cent. upon the average of former years, testified to the benefit of this return to primitive usage in the administration of Holy Baptism, "when the most number of people come together."

The first volume of our Parochial Registers (which date from 1601)
contains the following Dispensation from the Lenten Fast.

Hugh Gundrie, Minister or Curat of the parish of Ottery St. Mary within the county of Devon. To my well-beloved in Christ, Charles Vaughan, Esquire, now dwelling or remaining within the said parish of Ottery St. Marye, salutations: Whereas, I partly know of my own knowledge, and am credibly given to understand, that the eating of any fish is very hurtfull for your health, therefore that you may the better recover your health, as much as in me is, and by the lawe I may, I give and graunt unto you the said Charles Vaughan by these presents, license to eat flesh this present Lent ensuinge, and upon other days prohibited by the law; notwithstanding exhorting you to use this license and dispensation warily, so as no scandal grow thereby; and that you distribute, or cause to be distributed, the sum of six shillings and eight pence to the poor of the foresaid parish, according to the forme of the statute in that case made and provided. In witness whereof, I have hereunto put my hand and seale the first day of February, in the year of our Lord, 1634.

HUGH GUNDRIE, Ministr. ibid.
HUMPHREY SHEPPARD,
Churchwarden.

APPENDIX R.

Sir Walter Raleigh's House, and the Great House.

Nothing certain is known of Sir Walter Raleigh's connection with Ottery, but Polwhele, who published his *History of Devonshire* in 1793-7, speaks of the mouldering structure in which Sir Walter Raleigh once resided, and adds that there is "one turret still existing, and the house has altogether a monasterial appearance." It was the chief house of a block of five, which was consumed by fire on the 15th May, 1805. It stood on the ground now occupied by the side offices of Mr. Davy's residence in Mill street; and is described by those who remember it as rising above the adjoining houses, with stone mullioned windows and a projecting open porch, having a bench on either side within, and a chamber over, with a battlemented parapet. Polwhele probably alludes to this porch under the name of turret, for he is not always exact in his use of terms, as, for example, in his description of the Church, he calls the three sedilia within the Sacrarium, "three confessionals."

Another mansion, entitled "The Great House," which stood fronting the street in the garden north of the Church, was taken down early in the present century. It belonged latterly to the Saville family, but there is nothing known of its early history.

—

APPENDIX S.

Escot House (1680-1808).

Escot House was commenced by Sir Walter Yonge soon after his purchase of the estate in 1680, but not completed until after the Revolution in 1688. It was one of the most distinguished mansions in the neighbourhood, and was built by Inigo Jones, who also built Pynes, Franklyn, and many other houses in this county. There is a view of it, with plans, &c., published in *Vitruvius Britannicus*. Sir George Yonge (from whom it passed into the possession of Sir John Kennaway in 1794), supplied Mr. Polwhele with a particular account of the house, which is printed in a note to his history. It was "built of brick, with some stone ornaments, and formed an oblong square 90 feet by 80. All the offices under the house were 15, the ground-floor rooms 16, and the chamber floor 14 feet high; over which, were no less than sixteen rooms in the attics." King George III., with three of the Princesses, visited Sir George Yonge (the Secretary of War) there in 1789, when there was a vast concourse of all classes to give him a loyal welcome.

This splendid mansion was destroyed by fire on the 28th of December, 1808, in consequence of a lighted candle having been left in a dressing room, which set fire to the window curtains. The family, with a number of visitors, were at dinner between the hours of five and six, when the alarm was given; and so rapidly did the flames spread, that the mansion, together with the whole of the elegant furniture, valuable paintings, &c., was entirely destroyed; nothing being saved but the jewels, plate, and papers. A respectable yeoman of the neighbourhood, while endeavouring to render assistance, was killed by a fall from a ladder, leaving a widow and six children to lament his loss. The house was amply supplied with water contained in a large reservoir in the roof, and had the fire broken out in any of the lower rooms, in all probability the progress of the flames would have been arrested; but from its close proximity to the roof, the water supply could not be turned to account, and the melted lead soon fell in showers, rendering the interior of the house perfectly unapproachable.

The following extracts from his private journal show the humble spirit in which the pious master of the house desired to lay to heart this visitation: "A fire broke out at five o'clock in the chintze room while we were at dinner, and in about three hours and a half, the house was burnt to the ground, being uninsured. God's Holy Will be done!"

A few days afterwards, he writes thus: "This year ends so differently from former ones, having left me in a manner houseless, that a particular notice is due to it. I do not suppose that £25,000 would (especially at this time, when the price of timber is so high) replace the house and furniture as it before stood. May God of His infinite mercy sanctify it to me, and make this worldly loss conducive to my spiritual gain! I am deeply sensible of, and grateful for, the many blessings He has left me, and am rather doubtful if this house, while it stood, did not daily tempt me to break His Holy Commandment, 'Thou shalt not worship any graven image.'"

The first stone of the new house was laid by his infant grandson, John Henry Kennaway, on the 6th September, 1837. Escot park is extensive, and pleasantly diversified with wood and water. There is a tradition that John Locke often visited his friend Sir Walter Yonge here, to refresh himself after his close studies, and planned the various clumps, &c., of beech, and particularly the horse shoe, and the circular clump just above the silver firs.

APPENDIX T.

Belbury Castle, St. Michael's, West Hill.

Dr. Jeremiah Milles, the learned Dean of Exeter (1762-1784) and President of the Antiquarian Society, speaks of this entrenchment as "a small oval Danish fort;" but since archæology has been studied more systematically, the idea of ascribing to the Danes most of the camps of a circular or oval form has been exploded, and there is a greater disposition to regard them as British. Mr P. O. Hutchinson, who has bestowed great attention on the subject, and has personally examined all the hill fortresses and earth works of Eastern Devon, holds this opinion strongly, and has kindly allowed the following extract from his interesting Paper, read at the Meeting of the Archæological Association in Exeter in 1861, to be transferred to these pages : "Belbury Castle has been said to derive its name from Bel or Belus, the great Pagan Deity of old. This station, which occupied the crown of a hill one mile and a half south west from Ottery, was obliterated seventy years ago. On the last day of May, 1861, I assisted in exploring the site. After some inquiry, we found a man seventy-nine years of age, called Samuel White who lives at Castle Farm close by. He told us that when he was a boy, the hill was entirely open heath ; that seventy years ago, h and his late father were employed in leveling the entrenchments the camp, then entire; that they raised the earth in the interior with what they got at the encircling banks; that there was a great ditch all round outside; that the present road at the south and east sides occupies the bottom of the former ditch; that the camp was called Belbury, or Belsbury Castle; that he does not recollect any coins or other relics having been found in the locality; and that the field now standing in its place is called ' Castle Field.' This field is 230 paces long by 80 wide. We examined the remarkable sunk road running through the plantation on the west side of the hill, Samuel White said he could remember when it was perfect all the way northward to Street-way Head, and that even now, he could trace it in many places."

APPENDIX U.

Pixies' Parlour.

"The Pixies, in the superstition of Devonshire, are a race of beings invisibly small, and harmless or friendly to man. At a small distance from a village (Ottery St. Mary) in that county, half way up a wood-covered hill, is an excavation called the Pixies' Parlour. The roots of old trees form its ceiling; and on its sides are in-numerable cyphers, among which, the author discovered his own and those of his brothers, cut by the hand of childhood. At the foot of the hill flows the river Otter. To this place, the author, during the Summer months of the year 1793, conducted a party of young ladies; one of whom, of stature elegantly small, and of complexion colourless yet clear, was proclaimed the Faery Queen. On-which occasion, an irregular ode, entitled ' Songs of the Pixies,' was written." (*S. T. Coleridge's Preface to the Poem.*) Those who are attracted to the spot from its association with the poet's memory, will be glad to connect with it his touching " Sonnet to the River Otter," written after many eventful years of separation from the scenes of his childhood :

> Dear native brook! Wild streamlet of the West!
>   How many various-fated years have past,
>   What happy and what mournful hours, since last
> I skimmed the smooth thin stone along thy breast,
> Numbering its bright leaps! yet so deep imprest
> Sink the swee tscenes of childhood, that mine eyes
>   I never shut amid the sunny ray,
> But straight with all their tints thy waters rise,
>   Thy crossing plank, thy marge with willows grey,
> And bedded sand, that veined with various dyes,
> Gleamed through thy bright transparence! On my way,
>   Visions of childhood! oft have ye beguiled
> Lone manhood's cares, yet waking fondest sighs!
>   Ah! that once more I were a careless child!

G

APPENDIX V.

Clavering St. Mary, and Pendennis.

William Makepeace Thackeray, during his Charter House days (1825-8), used to spend part of his vacations at Larkbeare (on the confines of our parish), then occupied by his step-father, Major Carmichael Smyth ; and no person of these parts can read *Pendennis* without being struck with the impression which the scenery of this neighbourhood must have made upon his mind, to be reproduced in that remarkable story after a lapse of more than twenty years (1849). The local descriptions clearly identify Clavering St. Mary, Chatteris, and Baymouth with Ottery St. Mary, Exeter, and Sidmouth ; and, in the first edition, which was ornamented with vignettes in the margin, a sketch of the cock tower of the Church is introduced. In *Fraser's Magazine* for November, 1854, there is an article entitled *"Clavering St. Mary, and a Talk about Devonshire Worthies,"* which confirms this identity, where it speaks of "the birthplace of Pendennis, that 'little old town of Clavering St. Mary,' past which, the rapid river Brawl holds on its shining course, and which boasts a fine old Church with great grey towers, of which the sun illuminates the delicate carving, deepening the shadows of the deep buttresses, and gilding the glittering windows and flaming vane. Things have however changed at Clavering since Mr. Thackeray spent many a pleasant summer holiday there in his boyhood. The old Collegiate Church has been swept and garnished, and bedizened with finery until it scarcely knows itself; and the Wapshot boys no longer make a good cheerful noise, scuffling with their feet as they march into Church and up the organ-loft stairs, but walk demurely to their open seats in the side aisle." Mr. Thackeray was himself a contributor to *Fraser's Magazine* for many years (1834-1847), but is said to have closed his connection with that periodical with the Paper entitled *A Grumble about Christmas Books,* published in January, 1847.

APPENDIX W.

Ancient Mansions, &c., in the Parish.

(Communicated by LIEUT.-COLONEL HARDING, F.G.S., &c.)

1.

Cadhay, from its position and importance, claims our first notice. In the quaint words of Risdon (one of the best of fair Devon's historians) " it lieth west over the river Tale, which here unloadeth itself into the river Otter. It was once the residence of some so named, and came after unto one Robert Grenvill, whose daughter and heir, Joan, was married unto John Haydon, Esq., sometime Bencher of Lincoln's Inn, who builded at Cadhay a fair new house,* and enlarged his demesne." This John Haydon, a member of an ancient family, was second son of Richard, who died 13 Henry VIII. (1521), and descended from John Haydon de Boughwood, in Harpford parish, near Ottery, who was living there the 19th of King Edward II. (1325).

John Haydon, the first named, was born at Ebford, in the parish of Woodbury, and, dying at Cadhay, was buried on the north side of the Altar in the Church of Ottery, 1587. Prince says " that John Haydon was once married, but to whom is not quite clearly ascertained." The pedigree of the family, and Sir William Pole's *MS. History of Devon* inform us it was with Joan, daughter and heir of Robert Grenville, by Joan Cadhay, his wife, the daughter and heir of Cadhay, of Cadhay; but the inscription on his tomb describes her as Joan, cousin-german and heir of Joan Cadhay, who was the wife of Hugh Grenville, gent. Be this as it may, it appears evident that he died without issue, leaving his inheritance to Robert Haydon, the son of Thomas, his nephew. He married Christiana, daughter and heir of Robert Tidersleigh, of Tidersleigh, in Dorsetshire, leaving issue at his death Robert Haydon, who was living in 1620. He married Joan, eldest daughter of Sir Amias Pawlet, knight, and died, leaving Gideon Haydon his heir, who married Margaret, daughter of John Davy, of Creedy, by whom he had seven sons and five daughters. His eldest son and heir, Robert, succeeded to his inheritance at the age of 17.

The Haydons continued at Cadhay many descents; and it appears afterwards to have been purchased by William Peere Williams, Esq., Barrister-at-Law, and author of the Reports. He

* Cadhay is fortunate in having fallen into the hands of an owner, who, although necessarily non-resident, takes a laudable interest in the maintenance of his inheritance. The mansion is kept in perfect repair, and habitable condition; and if only the bad taste of a bygone generation could be reversed by the careful and judicious restoration of those portions which were unfortunately modernized about the middle of the last century, few houses of its class and antiquity would bear a comparison with it. The quaint Quadrangle (or Court of the Kings, as it is called, from the effigies of King Henry VIII. and his three sovereign children, which stand, one over each of the entrances in the centre of the sides of the quadrangle) is readily shown to strangers, and is well worth a visit.

died at Cadhay, in 1766, leaving two daughters, co-heiresses; one married Sir Robert Sutton; the other, Elizabeth, on the 22nd June, 1771, became the wife of Admiral Thomas Graves (afterwards Lord Graves) of Thanks, in Cornwall. Mrs. Williams, relict of W. P. Williams, continued to reside at Cadhay, and died there in 1792. On the death of Lord Graves, in 1802, Cadhay became the property of his eldest daughter, the wife of William Bagwell, Esq. (*Vide* page 18, Note), and upon her decease, it descended to her next sister Anne Elizabeth, who married Sir Thomas Hare, Bart., of Norfolk. Their son, the present baronet of the same name, succeeded to the property. Some years ago, there was at Cadhay a curious picture of John Haydon and Joan his wife, where John was represented on one side of an Altar, together with his sons kneeling, and Joan with her daughters on the other side, all in the attitude of prayer. This picture is supposed to be still in the possession of some member of the family. The Ottery branch of the Haydon family is represented by Mr. Frank Scott Haydon, of the Record Office.

2.

Knightstone, another ancient mansion, lies south of Ottery. The house is entered by a porch which leads to a hall 26 feet long by 20 in breadth. This room, owing to its two transomed windows, may, in some degree, be compared to Holcombe court, in the parish of Holcombe Rogus. The ceiling appears to conceal an open roof, but as access could not be obtained to it, its existence could not be ascertained. The chimney of the hall bears the date 1567, when the house was erected by Gideon Sherman. The front is covered with creepers, which interfere with the display of its architecture; and modern barge boards are attached to each gable.

Knightstone had originally lords so named. We learn from Risdon that "about 44 Edward III.—Richard, son of John de Knightston, conveyed this land to Thomas Bittlesgate, who made his dwelling there," unto whom Margaret, the wife of John Upton, (sister to the above Richard,) and Elias Upton, her son, made a release thereof. Here Thomas Bittlesgate resided in October, 1381; as we learn by Bishop Brantyngham's register, that licence was granted to Thomas Bittlesgate, and Jane his wife, "Oratoria sive Capellas infra maneria sua de Kyngeston (Knightstone), infra Parochiam de Otry Sancte Marie, et de Sparkeye, infra Parochiam de Coleton situat." Knightstone was entailed on him and his children, with remainder to William, Lord Bonvill. All the children died without issue, and this inheritance, on the death of Lord Bonvill, (who was beheaded at St. Alban's, in the last year of Henry VI., 1461), descended to Cicelie, his only daughter and heir.[*] She was the wife of Thomas Grey, Marquis

---

[*] We learn from Risdon and others, that Anthony Widville, Lord Rivers, laid claim to Knightstone as next heir of Bittlesgate. The family of Widville, in Northamptonshire has an early origin, for when Robert Fallot certified his knight's fees, *temp.* Henry II., Willielmus de Widville is there mentioned as holding of the said Robert, half a knight's fee in the county of Northampton. (See Hearne's *Liber Niger*

of Dorset, who died 22 Henry VIII., 1530, leaving a son, Henry Grey, Duke of Suffolk, by whose attainder in February, 1554,† this land fell to the crown, and Queen Mary granted Shute and Wiscomb, the principal residences of the Bonville family, to Sir William Petre, Her Majesty's Secretary of War; but Knightstone was purchased by Mr. William Sherman, a merchant of Ottery, who died in 1583. His effigies, in brass, together with that of his father John, and Richard his son, by a second marriage with Joan, the daughter of John Mallett, of Axminster, still remain in Ottery Church, at the entrance to the Chapel of St. Stephen, which, it is said, belonged to the estate. The family of Coplestone succeeded to the property by marriage with the heiress of the Shermans, and from them this estate came, by purchase, to Hawtrey. The Rev. Dr. Drury purchased it of the Trustees appointed under the will of Stephen Hawtrey, Esq., in 1803. His son, the Rev. Charles Drury, restored the hall and rooms leading from it in 1837; previous to which the windows were blocked up, and it was used for farm purposes. He died very recently, and bequeathed it to his great nephew Mr. Gerald Drury, the son of the late Archdeacon Drury, sometime Chaplain of the House of Commons.

3.

Ash, another ancient mansion, situated near the high road leading from Honiton to Exeter, and on the north side of the parish of Ottery, was in Henry III.'s time belonging to Robert de Lupo, or Wolfe, whom John de Lupo succeeded in Edward I.'s time; from whence it passed to Treley, in which name it continued divers descents, when it was sold to Bonville, and by the attainder of the Duke of Suffolk, it passed to the Crown. It was afterwards in possession of Mr. Humphry Walrond, a younger branch of the Bradfield family, and from thence it passed to Rev. Mr. Bennett. Ultimately, it came to Rev. Thomas Putt, of Coombe, in Gittisham parish, and descended to Rev. Thomas John Marker by his bequest. His son, Richard Marker, Esq., of Coombe, is the present proprietor.

5

Holcombe (probably from hollow-comb) is a short distance north of Ottery, and was sometime in the family of Malherbe. Towards the latter end of the reign of Henry VI., John Moore, a man of some quality, dwelt there, in whose name and posterity it continued to the commencement of Queen Elizabeth's reign. It was mortgaged and forfeited to John Eveleigh, Esq., Feodary and a Justice of the Peace, who seated himself there, and it was the dwelling of Mr. George Eveleigh, the son of John, in Sir William

Saccarii). In 1448 (26 Henry VI.), Sir Richard Widville was created a Baron of the Realm by the title of Lord Rivers, and in the 5th Edward IV. he was raised to the dignity of an Earl by the same title.

† The mutilation of the arms in the north porch of the Church, may have taken place in consequence of the attainder of the Duke of Suffolk; but Dr. Oliver suggests that the mutilated arms were probably those of the Duke of Somerset, to whom the Manor and Church were granted by King Henry VIII., and that they were effaced on his subsequent attainder.

Pole's time (*cir.* 1606). In 1797 it was held by the heirs of John Leigh, Esq., and afterwards by the Misses Anderson. It became, by marriage, the property of Captain Charles Grant, R.N., from whose family it has lately been purchased by Mr. Elias Pidsley, the present occupier.

6

Thorne, in Ottery parish, lies west of the river Otter. John Thorn held this land in King John's time, Walter or Gualterus de Spineto in the reign of Henry III., and Roger A' Thorn in the time of Edward III., who died without issue, and his sister Jane brought it to Henry Cooke, her husband, whose father was a citizen of Exeter. His posterity remained there many years until the succession of Richard Cooke, who was born in 1607. He appears to have died without issue,[*] and the property was sold in several ties, when parts of it fell into the hands of Rolfe, Vivian, and Pitfield. Rolfe had a mortgage on a part or the whole of the estate, and he bequeathed the amount he had advanced to the Trustees of the Episcopal Schools at Exeter, founded by Offspring Blackall, Lord Bishop of Exeter, and they entered into possession in 1744.

7

The barton of *Bishop's Court*, said to be one of four seats held by Bishop Grandisson, was leased to the family of Mercer in Edward III.'s time. Bishop Grandisson granted a lease for lives to John Mercer, who was his steward, and it continued to be held by the family until the reign of Henry VIII., who seized this inheritance and gave it, together with Tavistock Abbey and other lands in Devon, to the Earl of Bedford, under whose family the Mercers continued to hold the property until the reign of James I., when they purchased the fee from them. This estate has descended in lineal succession, and was held in jointure by the widow of the Rev. Henry Marker (whose grandmother was heiress of the Mercers), and the property is now held by her grandson, Richard Marker, Esq., of Coombe, in the parish of Gittisham.

8

Before I close my sketch of this interesting neighbourhood, I would mention some ancient British and Roman remains still extensively existing in Ottery parish. It has been supposed that the river Otter, which runs through the vale of Honiton, formed a frontier defence between two frontier tribes, the Dunmonii and Morini, or, as at present exists, between Devonshire and Dorsetshire. There is evidence of this in the form and position of the fortresses which command the valleys toward the west, and especially from the evident traces upon the hills, of ancient track-ways connecting them on their eastern sides. Of the remains thus alluded to I would particularly mention Belbury Castle (Appendix T),

---

[*] The last of the Cooke family married Trosse; his father, Sherman; and his grandfather, Coplestone.

Farway Castle, and Sidbury Castle, in the neighbourhood of Ottery.

Farway Castle is a circular entrenchment, 200 feet in diameter, and situated on the flat of the hill, commanding extensive views on almost all sides.

Sidbury Castle is the largest area in the neighbourhood, but not so strongly fortified. It is of a peculiar form, being pear-shaped, with the principal entrance at the north-west end and the narrowest part of the work. It is 1,400 feet long, and strengthened by an entire double ditch. A popular belief exists that a large amount of treasure is buried there, and it goes by the name of treasury, or, " money heap."

On the East hill, near Ottery, are several British barrows. The old British and Roman Keneld-way, or Icening street (deriving its name from the Iceni), passes through this parish. The main line from Honiton to Exeter was formerly to be traced, in perfect condition, forsome distance at Fair-mile.* An eminent antiquary, (Dr. Stukely) a century since, stated that it was the noblest piece of road he had ever seen. A branch of this road passed from Colyford, over Farway hill, through the town of Ottery, and by Straight-gate farm to join the main-line at Street-way head.

Many coins, both Greek and Roman, have been found in this neighbourhood.

APPENDIX X.

The Geology of Ottery St. Mary and its Neighbourhood.

(Communicated by the Rev. R. Kirwan, m.a., Rector of Gittisham.)

I propose to append a few remarks on the physical geology of the parish of Ottery St. Mary and the surrounding country, inasmuch as this district possesses ample materials to engage the attentive and careful examination of the geologist.

The town itself is situate in a depression of the range known as the Black Down hills, which, having the vale of Taunton on the northern escarpment, and that of Cullompton on the west, form an almost continuous line extending in a west and south west direction as far as Exmouth. In fact the whole of the high land between Golden Cap hill, near Lyme Regis on the west, and the Haldons on the east, forms geologically a portion of this same Black Down range of hills. Throughout its entire extent it exhibits decisive manifestations of denudation. Not only have the ridges and summits of the hills been removed by denuding causes so as now to form a table-land, but their surface is furrowed by coombes and ravines, which unite and terminate in valleys that intersect the range in a direction chiefly north and south, and form outlets for the rivers that flow from the interior of

* Dr. Musgrave of Exeter in his *Belgium Britannicum*, states that he considers the traces of the military road most certain between Axminster and Honiton, and particularly the *Milliare aureum*, or golden mile-mark or pillar, as he describes Fair Mile, Far, *Saxon*, a road.

the country into the British Channel. The course of the smaller excavations or coombes is exceedingly various, but their general bearing is east and west; they gradually increase in breadth as they descend, and frequently their opposite sides have corresponding curves and angles; this appearance, however, is not observable in the principal valleys. The surface-soil of these hills is subject to considerable variation. On the summit it is usually shallow, the substratum is generally a tenacious yellow clay, whilst over this there occurs a layer of angular masses of chert and chalk flints, with a slight covering of vegetable mould. Among the more elevated ridges there is sometimes merely a covering of flints, upon which the turf grows spontaneously.

For the information of the general reader it may be necessary to remark that here, as elsewhere, in every instance the strata maintain a certain fixed superposition, and that however great the displacement or interruption, this order is never inverted. To illustrate this remark, I may observe that the *lias*, which separates the chalk and associated strata from the new red sandstone in the neighbourhood of Lyme Regis, is altogether wanting at Ottery St. Mary, and indeed throughout Devonshire; but in these instances, the cretaceous beds repose immediately upon the new red sandstone, the relative position of the masses remaining unaltered by the absence of the intervening deposit.

By reference to any geological map, it will be observed that the higher parts of the Black Down hills, of which it will be remembered the East and West hills of Ottery St. Mary form a portion, consist of the deposit known geologically as *green sand*, and which here attains an average thickness of about 100 feet, whilst the valleys between the hill-slopes consist of the clays and marls that constitute the new red sandstone series.

The following arrangement of the strata will be found to accord with their natural order of succession:

Formations.	Sub-divisions.	Localities.
I. TERTIARY.	Various beds of sand, marl, and plastic clay, and of gravel formed of unrolled chalk flints.	Summits and slopes of the Black Down hills.
II. CHALK.	i. Upper chalk with flints. ii. Lower chalk without flints.	White Cliff, Beer; Dowlands; and as far west as Duncombe, 1 mile east from Sidmouth.
III. GREEN-SAND.	i. Brown sandstone. ii. Concretionary layers of harder sandstone. iii. Sandstone with green earth. iv. Sandstone with chert seams.	The higher portions of the Black Down range including East and West hills, Ottery St. Mary.
IV. LIAS.	Alternations of blueish green and light-coloured slaty marls.	Lyme Regis, and the country between Chard and Axminster.
V. NEW RED SANDSTONE.	Red marls and conglomerates mixed with others that are blue, green, and of different light-colored tints.	Coast between Seaton and Lyme Regis; also that between Sidmouth and Dawlish; also the valleys between the ranges of hills, including that in which Ottery St. Mary is situate.

A physical characteristic of this locality should here be pointed out, in as much as it is due to the geological constitution of the soil. I refer to the barren aspect of the hill-sides in the upper, as compared with the lower portion of their escarpments. The chief products of the upper portions are fern, heather, and furze; whilst upon the lower portions sunny pastures, smiling corn fields, and blooming orchards everywhere abound. The line of demarcation between the barren and the fertile portions of the hill-sides is by no means regular, if we may judge by the uneven line presented by the hedgerows. When the rich loams formed by the red marls of the new red sandstone run far up the hill-sides there the corn flourishes; where, on the other hand, the hungry beds of the green sandstone series strike down into the valley, the contrast is conspicuous.

MINERALS.

In the immediate neighbourhood of Ottery St. Mary the minerals are but few in number, and comprise but one metalliferous ore.

1. Crystallised quartz. This is of frequent occurrence in the cavities of siliceous nodules, &c. The form of the crystals is that of a six-sided pyramid; whilst their colours vary from reddish brown to light blue, grey and white.

2. Chalcedony is often found occupying the hollows of flints. In some cases the flint passes insensibly into chalcedony, whilst in others, the line of demarcation is distinctly visible.

3. Calcareous spar, often found in the fissures and hollows of the red marls.

4. Iron pyrites occurs very commonly in globular and in irregular masses in the green sand that (as has been stated) forms the capping deposit of the East and West hills. The interior of these masses exhibits a radiated structure, and possesses a brilliant metallic lustre. The mineral occasionally encloses flints, shells, echinites, &c., and sometimes fills up the cavities of the latter. Along the coast of East Devon it occurs so abundantly that it becomes an article of commerce. It is collected and sent to Plymouth, where the sulphur is extracted from it, and employed in the preparation of sulphuric acid.

APPENDIX Y.

*A List of the Rarer British Plants, in the Parish of
Ottery St. Mary.*

(Communicated by GEORGE BUCHANAN WOLLASTON, Esq.)*

Class I., DICOTYLEDONES.

Subclass 1, *Exogenæ.*
Subdivision 1, *Thalamifloræ.*

Order, Ranunculaceæ.
Ranunculus fluitans   Mill stream.
,.   arvensis   Cornfields.

Order, Nymphæaceæ.
Nymphæa alba, White water lily
       Ornamental waters.
Nuphar lutea   Ditto.

Order, Cruciferæ.
Cheiranthus Cheiri, Wall-flower
       On the Church.
Barbarea præcox   West hill.
Teesdalia nudicaulis   Ditto.
Thlaspi arvense, Penny cress, Ridgeway.
Senebiera Coronopus   St. Saviours.

Order, Violaceæ.
Viola palustris, Marsh violet
       West hill.
 ,,   lactea, White violet
       Watery lane, &c.

Order, Droseraceæ.
Drosera rotundifolia, Round-
leaved sundew   West hill.
Drosera longifolia, Long-leaved
sundew   West hill.

Order, Hypericineæ.
Hypericum Androsæmum, Tutsan
       East and West hills, &c.
 ,,   elódes   Bogs, West hill.

Order, Geranaceæ.
Geranium lucidum, Shining Cranes-
bill   Sidmouth road, &c.

Order, Lineæ.
Linum augustifolium   East hill.
 ,,   usitatissimum, Common flax
       Cultivated fields.

Order, Oxalideæ.
Oxalis Acetosella, Wood sorrel
       Shady woods.
 ,,   stricta   West hill, rare.

Order, Leguminosæ.
Ulex nanus, Autumnal Furze
       East and West hill.
Genista Anglica, Needle Whin
       West hill.

Order, Rosaceæ.
Agrimonia odorata
       Near Pixies' parlour, (very rare.)
Fragaria elatior, Hautboy Strawberry
       Woods, West hill.

Order, Crassulaceæ.
Cotyledon Umbilicus
       Universally distributed.

Order, Grossularieæ.
Ribes Grossularia, Gooseberry
       Knightstone, &c.

Order, Saxifrageæ.
Saxifraga granulata   East hill.
Chrysosplenium oppositifolium,
    Golden Saxifrage   Great Well.

Order, Umbelliferæ.
Helosciadium inundatum
       Mill-stream, rare.
Conium maculatum   By the river.

Order, Araliaceæ.
Adoxa moschatellina
       Woods and shady banks.

Order, Loranthaceæ.
Viscum album, Mistletoe
       On apple trees.

Order, Rubiaceæ.
Rubia peregrina, Wild madder
       East hill, &c.

* To Mr. Wollaston (an old *Alumnus* of the King's School), the parish is indebted
for the beautiful designs for St. Michael's Church and Parsonage, on West Hill, and for
the National Schools in the town.

Order, Compositæ.
Solidago Virgaurea, Golden rod
          Various places.
Tenacetum vulgare, Tansy, Way-sides,
Serratula tinctoria, Saw-wort
        Woods and shady banks.
Hieraceum prenanthoides
        Woods and shady banks.
   „   umbellatum
        Woods and shady banks.

Order, Campanulaceæ.
Jasione montana, Sheep's scabious
       East and West hill, &c.
Campanula Trachelium, Nettle-
  leaved bell flower   Roadsides.
Wahlenbergia hederacea, Ivy-
  leaved Bell Flower, Bogs, West hill.

Order, Ericaceæ.
Vaccinium Oxycoccos, Cranberry
        Bogs, West hill.

Order, Apocynea.
Vinca minor, Periwinkle
        Near Gosford, &c.

Order, Menyanthideæ.
Menyanthes trifoliata, Buckbean,
        Bogs, West hill.

Order, Boragineæ.
Anchusa sempervirens   Tiphill head.

Order, Solanaceæ.
Datura Stramonium, Thorn-Apple
        Waste ground

Order, Scrophularineæ.
Antirrhinum Orontium
       Dry gravelly fields.
Linaria Cymbalaria, Ivy-leaved
  Toad flax,   Churchyard wall.
Veronica Buxbaumii Cultivated land.

Order, Lentibulariaceæ.
Pinguicula vulgaris, Butterwort
       Bogs, West hill.
   „   Lusitanica   Ditto.

Order, Primulaceæ.
Lysimachia vulgaris River side (rare).

Order, Chenopodiaceæ.
Chenopodium Bonus-Henricus
       Near the town.

Order, Polygonaceæ.
Rumex sanguineus In the Town (rare).
Polygonum Bistorta, Snakeweed
       Near the river.

Order, Urticaceæ.
Parietaria diffusa, Pellitory of
  the wall   Churchyard wall.
Humulus Lupulus, Hop
      Hedge near Gosford, &c.

Class II., MONOCOTYLEDONES.

Order, Orchideæ.
Orchis Morio, Green-winged
  Meadow O.   Moist meadows.
  „ mascula, Early purple O.
      Woods and hedge banks.
Habenaria chlorantha, Great
  Butterfly O.   Woods.
Listera ovata, Twayblade   Ditto.
Epipactis latifolia   Near Escot.

Order, Irideæ.
Iris Pseudacorus, Yellow Flag
      By the river.
  „ foetidissima Cliff by ditto, &c.

Order, Amaryllideæ.
Narcissus biflorus   S. Saviours.
  „ Pseudo narcissus, Daffodil
     Orchards, lanes, &c.

Order, Liliaceæ.
Allium ursinum, Ramsons
     By the river, &c.

Order, Juncaceæ.
Narthecium ossifragum, Bog Asphodel
      Bogs, West hill.
Juncus squarrosus   Ditto.

Order, Cyperaceæ.
Rhynchospora alba   Ditto.
Eriophorum polystachion, Cotton-
  grass   Ditto.
Carex pulicaris   Ditto.
  „ vulpina   Ditto.
  „ paniculata   Ditto.
  „ stellulata   Ditto.

Order, Gramineæ.
Apera Spica-venti Sandy fields, rare.
Phragmites communis River banks.
Melica uniflora   Shady woods, &c.
  „ cærulea East and West hills.
Poa nemoralis   Woods.
Festuca ovina, β vivipara
      Bogs, West hill.
Nardus stricta, Mat-grass Ditto.

CLASS III., CRYPTOGRAMÆ DUCTULOSÆ.

Order, Equisitaceæ.
Equisetum sylvaticum

Order, Filices.
Suborder, Polypodiaceæ.
Polypodium vulgare   Universal.
    „   „ var. bifidum   „
Lastrea montana, Sweet mountain Fern
                East and West hills, &c.
   „   filix-mas, Male Fern
                Universally distributed.
   „   pseudo-mas (Wollaston) False
         Mas, Universally distributed.
   „   „   var. furcillata, Rill.
   „   dilatata, Broad Fern
                East and West hills.
   „   spinulosa, Prickly Fern
                East hill (rare).
   „   æmula, Hay-scented Fern
                Ditto (ditto.)
Polystichum aculeatum
            Sparingly everywhere.
   „   setiferum (Forskal, 1755)
                Universal.
   „   „   var. plumosum
   „   „   „ cristatum
   „   „   „ gracile
   „   „   „ lineare
   „   „   „ decurrens
   „   „   „ cristato-gracile
                Jacksoni
   „   „   „ inæquale
   „   „   „ varians
   „   „   „ præmorsum
   „   „   „ grandidens
   „   „   „ pterophorum
   „   „   „ alatum
   „   „   „ retroflexum
   „   „   „ ramosum
   „   „   „ flexuosum
   „   „   „ proliferum Wollastonii
   „   „   „ proliferum
                Wollastonii, No. 2

   „   „   „ acutilobum
   „   „   „ divisilobum
                Wollastonii
   „   „   „ serrulatum
   „   „   „ crispato-rotundum
   „   „   „ venoso-variegatum
   „   „   „ exile
[All these varieties have been found
   in the Parish, and many others of
   less note.]
Athyrium Filix-fœmina, Lady fern
                Common.
   „   „ var. subcristatum
                West Hill.
Asplenium Adiantum-nigrum, Black
   Spleenwort   Common.
   „   Trichomanes, Common
   Spleenwort   Churchyard wall, and
                East and West hills.
   „   Ruta-muraria, Wall Rue
                Ditto.
Scolopendrium vulgare Harts-
            tongue, Common
   „   var. marginatum
   „   „ muricatum
   „   „ variegatum
   „   „ crispum
   „   „ sagittato-crispum
[All these varieties have been found
   in the Parish].
Blechnum spicans (Wollaston)
   Hard Fern   Common.
Pteris aquilina, Brakes   Everywhere.
   „   „ var. cristata
            Moor lane and West hill.
Osmunda regalis, Royal Fern   Ditto.
Ophioglossum vulgatum, Adders-
   tongue   Moist meadows.

Order, Lycopodiaceæ.
Lycopodium inundatum
            Bogs, West hill.

APPENDIX Z.

Miscellaneous Statistics, &c., of the Parish and Neighbourhood.

(A.)

The area of the Parish, under the Census Return of 1861, amounts to 9470 acres. The extent of the Parish, according to the Tithe-Apportionment Map, is set down at 9944a. 2r. 4p., including roads and rivers. The length of roads, traversing this area, is estimated at 60 miles.

(B.)

Population Return of the whole parish - - 4340

Sub-Divisions.

District of Tipton - - - 470

District of Escot (exclusive of 70 from Talaton) - 464

District of St. Michael, about - - 350

Residue of the Parish, including the conventional District of Alfington - - - - 3056

(C.)

Church Accommodation.

	Appropriated		Free		Total
St. Mary's	444	..	556	..	1000
St. John's	104	..	206	..	310
St. Philip and St. James's	100	..	110	..	210
St. Michael's ..	..	..	192	..	192
St. James the Great ..	..	..	120	..	120
	648	..	1184	..	1832

(D.)

Extent of Burial Grounds including the Sites of the several Churches.

				A.	R.	P.
St. Mary's Churchyard	..	..	..	1	1	16
St. John's ..	..	..	..	1	0	14
St. Philip & St. James's	..	..	..		1	22
St. Michael's ..	..	..	..		2	8

(E).

The Parish Registers.

The Register of Burials commences .. 16th May, ⎫
,,   Baptisms ,,   .. 28th ,,   ⎬ 1603
,,   Marriages ,,   .. 28th August, ⎭

(F.)

Assignment of Ecclesiastical Districts.

1.

District assigned to the Church of St. John the Evangelist at Tipton under the 16th Section of 59 George III., cap. 134, by Order in Council held 8th day of May, 1841, and published in the *London Gazette*, July 16th, 1841.

2.

District assigned to the Church of St. Philip and St. James the Less, at Escot, by Her Majesty's Commissioners for Building New Churches, under the 10th Section of 1 & 2 Gul. IV., cap. 58, Dated 11th June, 1844.

3.

District assigned to the Church of St. Michael the Archangel, on West Hill, by Order in Council published in the *London Gazette*, in pursuance of the Act of 59 George III., cap. 130, and 2 & 3 Victoria, cap. 49, A.D. 1857.

(G.)

Tithe Apportionment (14th April, 1842).

Award of Rent-Charge to the Chapter of Windsor in lieu of Great Tithes £995 15 0

Rent-Charge to the Church Corporation in lieu of the Small Tithes £250 12 10

(H.)

Water Supply of the Town.

Provision is made for an average allowance of twenty gallons daily, to each individual in the town. "The quality of the water, as respects hardness, is 10°, and it may be described as softer than the generality of waters."—*Report to the General Board Health, by T. W. Rammell, Esq., Superintending Inspector.*

(I.)

Rainfall of the District.

The Climate has, to the full extent, the mildness prevailing over all the lower parts of the South Eastern Coast; but the Returns of the Rainfall do not exhibit the excess of humidity generally found to accompany here this advantage. Observations by Dr. Cullen, on the neighbouring town of Sidmouth, during the four years, 1844-7, show a mean annual depth of 26.07 inches only.— *Report to the General Board of Health, &c.*

Events of Local Interest in their Chronological Order.

The Manor of Ottery given by King Edward the Confessor to the
Chapter of St. Mary, Rouen .. .. .. A.D. 1061

A new Parish Church consecrated by Bishop Bronescombe .. 1260

The Manor and Church conveyed by the Chapter of Rouen to Bishop
Grandisson .. .. 13th June, 1335

Date of Endowment Deed of the College .. .. 22nd January, 1337-8

Conveyance of lands by John Laurence to Feoffees for the relief of the
poor 1440

Bequest of 146 books, mostly written with his own hand, to the Church
by John de Exeter .. .. .. 28th July, 1445

King Henry VI. received with great solemnity by the Canons of the
College, where he lodged two nights .. .. 14th July, 1451

King Henry VII. visited Ottery on the termination of Perkin War-
beck's Insurrection .. .. .. 3rd November, 1497

The College dissolved by King Henry VIII., and a Charter granted to
Four Governors .. .. .. 24th December, 1545

Date of Gift of Henry Beaumont to the Feoffees for the poor of Ottery
17th March, 1590

King Charles I. passed from Honiton to Exeter .. 26th July, 1644

The town occupied by the Parliamentary troops under General Fairfax
28th October-2nd December, 1645

The Prince of Orange (afterwards King William III.) dined at Ottery
on his way from Exeter to Axminster* .. 21st November, 1688

A Parish Workhouse (to contain 200) ordered to be erected "by the
Hospital" near St. Saviour's Bridge 1738

"Great Fire" in the town .. .. .. 16th March, 1767

First stone of the Factory laid by Sir George Yonge, Bart., and John
Duntze, Esq.† 1788

King George III. and three Princesses visited Escot on their way from
Weymouth to Exeter .. .. .. 13th August, 1798

The temporary Barracks on West Hill built 1803

Cadhay Bridge and Feniton Bridge washed away by a flood .. 1808

The Parish School established 1813

Public rejoicings during three successive days for the Peace of Paris June, 1814

The temporary Barracks taken down 1814

The Manor of Ottery conveyed by J. M. How, Esq., to Sir John
Kennaway Bart. .. .. .. October, 1822

The Factory converted from a woollen to a silk Factory .. 1823

Gosford Bridge washed away by a flood .. .. 4th October, 1824

Great Storm on the Coast of Devon and Cornwall .. 23rd November, 1824

Organ erected in the Parish Church under a faculty .. July, 1828

The Parish Workhouse closed and Union-house at Honiton opened 1838

Public rejoicings for the Queen's Coronation .. 28th June, 1838

First stone of Escot Church laid by Sir John Kennaway, Bart., 3rd August, 1838

---

* Part of his army had been stationed here during his stay at the Deanery in Exeter.
† Originally for the manufacture of Serge known as "long ells," for the East India
Company.

First stone of Tipton Church laid by Archdeacon Moore-Stevens
17th August, 1838

District Churches consecrated: Tipton, 29th April, and Escot 1st May 1840

Tipton Churchyard consecrated..   3rd April, 1843

Ruridecanal Chapter of the Clergy of the Deanery of Aylesbeare held
in the Lady Chapel   2nd December, 1844

Passed through the Post Office, 79,127 letters, 12,209 newspapers in the
year   1844

First stone of St. Michael's Church, West Hill, laid by Sir J. T.
Coleridge   6th October, 1845

Consecration of St. Michael's Church   29th September, 1846

Restoration of the Parish Church commenced 21st May   1849

The Church of St. James the Great at Alfington opened under the
Bishop's License*   11th August, 1849

St. Saviour's Bridge washed away by a flood   20th December, 1849

Opening Services in the Parish Church after the Restoration 14th May, 1850

Order of Council for establishing the Local Board of Health 13th July, 1850

Water supply brought into the town   1852

New appointment of Trustees of the Feoffee Charities 26th January, 1854

Order in Council, prohibiting Interments in the Parish Church 18th October, 1854

Town Hall opened ..   10th April, 1860

The Volunteer Rifle Corps established   14th June, 1860

The South Western Railway from Honiton to Exeter opened for traffic
19th July, 1860

The Provident Dispensary established   1860

The Act for the Sidmouth Railway and Harbour Company received the
Royal assent   7th August, 1862

Public Rejoicings for the Marriage of the Prince of Wales 10th March, 1863

Shock of an Earthquake felt at 3·30 a.m. ..   6th October, 1863

First Meeting of the East Devon Choral Association held in the Parish
Church   2nd August, 1864

The town lighted with Gas   —— 1865

Great Fire consuming 111 houses   25th May, 1866

Disastrous Fall of a Chimney, causing the death of eight persons
2nd September, 1866

Eastern Entrance to the Churchyard opened 3rd February, 1867

The new Girls' School Room (built by Sir J. T. Coleridge) opened
13th March, 1867

The new Boys' School opened ..   24th June, 1868

Slight Shock of an Earthquake felt at 10·55 p.m. 30th October, 1868

The first Poll for a County Election taken at Ottery 23rd November, 1 8

---

* The site was purchased, and the Church, together with a residence for the Minister, and a School-house (after designs by Mr. Butterfield) built by Sir J. T. Coleridge; who also provides a stipend for the Minister, and maintains the school.

WILLIAM POLLARD, PRINTER, 58, NORTH STREET, EXETER.

K. 3.